What A Bride Wants

What A Bride Wants

A MONTANA BORN BRIDES NOVELLA

KELLY HUNTER

TULE
PUBLISHING

DEDICATION

To Jane Porter and the wonderful gang at Tule Publishing. Thanks for your laughter, the endless encouragement, and for the opportunity to come play in Marietta.

Dear Reader,

Writing into a pre-built fictional world is always a challenge and a pleasure. The small town of Marietta, Montana has been crafted with such love and care, and the people that inhabit it are so real to me now that I want to sit down to drinks and a meal with them at Grey's Saloon. I want to eat Sage Carrigan's salted toffee on a regular basis and stroll through Bramble Park in the summertime and in the snow. I just want to live there.

The Great Wedding Giveaway is a Marietta Chamber of Commerce initiative, aimed at bringing tourists to the town and encouraging a thriving destination wedding trade. In *What A Bride Wants,* we see the launch of the Great Wedding Giveaway during a Valentine's Day Ball (see our Pinterest boards for more). My heroine enters my couple in the wedding giveaway as an act of support for her hero, and united they stand in the face of great turmoil and danger. Will they win the competition?

I don't think they can wait that long.

I hope you enjoy Ella and Sawyer's story, and then look forward to the rest of our Montana Born Brides.

Happy Reading,
Kelly Hunter

Chapter One

"YES, I KNOW he's perfectly presentable and possibly a very nice person. Second-born son from a good ranching family. All good things. It's just that when he looks at me he sees Emerson Holdings and award-winning bloodlines – money on the hoof. He doesn't see *me*."

Ella Grace Emerson leaned against the walnut desk and watched with fond exasperation as her father paced the length of his study. He stopped and stooped to add another block of wood to the fire that sat snug within the stonework of the study's western wall. A huge picture window took up most of another wall and in the distance loomed the soaring, snow-clad Crazy Mountains of Montana.

The charity dinner they'd just returned from had dragged on late into the evening. They'd been seated at a table of eight that had included Joe Carter and his middle son Max, and the blatant matchmaking efforts of both fathers had been enough to set Ella's teeth on edge.

Max's half-baked interest in her good-self had done the rest.

"It was worth a try," her father argued. "You and Max have similar social status, similar interests. It *could* have worked well."

"That's what you always say. And it never does. Daddy, I am *not* a cow to be bred. You need to let me find my own man."

"But you *don't*." Samuel T. Emerson threw up his hands. They were good hands, big and scarred and strong. They'd picked her up over the years and held her tight when she'd come off a horse. When her mother had died. When her high school crush hadn't invited her to the prom. "Where are you going to find this man, Ella Grace? Out here with the cattle? Roaming around Marietta? Livingston, maybe? At least Livingston has more variety than Marietta, but wait… you never go there. You're buried here. You could travel anywhere. Canada. Australia. Europe. But you don't. You haven't had a holiday in three years."

"Has it really been that long?"

"Ella Grace, you're twenty-five—"

"Hardly on the shelf."

"—And opinionated as all get out, for which I take complete responsibility."

"Surely I should take *some*—

"And I would see you happily settled before I die."

"I am happy. And I don't feel at all unsett—" She broke off as his words filtered through, and stood up hastily so that she could keep him in view as he headed for the sideboard and the crystal decanters of liquor that lived there. She eyed him worriedly, tried to look closer, but was hampered by flickering firelight and a face full of shadows. "Wait. Dad, are you sick? Is that what all this is about? You're *dying*?"

"No! No faster than the next man. Lord, Ella, but you'd test the patience of a saint." Her father poured himself a hefty two fingers worth of bourbon and downed the liquid in one long swallow.

"Where's mine?"

"You're not the one second guessing everything you're about to say." He put down the cut-crystal glass and turned to face her, his blue eyes not nearly as bright as they'd once been. He seemed to stoop a little, his suit sat his shoulders more loosely than it once had, and it dawned on Ella that, sick or not, her father was getting old. "Ella Grace, I've spoiled you rotten. You're used to giving orders and having them obeyed. You'd cut a man down as quick as look at him, especially if you know that he has ranching interests of his own. Why do you do that? I've taught you everything I know about cattle production and ranching, and I know you love this life and this land. Max would have been a good fit for you and the business both, but you made no effort with him tonight at all. None."

"You're wrong. Max and I both made an effort to get to know each other at the start of the evening, but there was no spark." Did she really have to spell it out for him? "Isn't this my prettiest dress?" The gown was several years old, but still stylish enough to make her feel good about wearing it. It made the most of her breasts and showcased her toned and slender arms. It cut in at the waist and out again to fall softly over her hips. It was neither too sexy nor too old-fashioned. The color was a deep and luscious scarlet and suited her creamy skin and dark brown hair to perfection. Ella *had* made an effort to dress well tonight. She'd even worn jewelry and that practically *never* happened. "Don't I look presentable?"

"You look beautiful," her father offered gruffly.

"And," Ella smelled her wrist and wafted it gently in her father's direction, "I smell like gardenias. And Max smelled good too and looked very presentable, but there was no attraction between us. And if there's no chemistry now, what with both of us looking our best and being on our best behavior, what hope is there for chemistry later on? Daddy, I want the spark. The lightning bolt." *The lust.* "And then once that's in place I'll see what I can do when it comes to cultivating the love."

"I so wish your mother was here."

"Daddy, please—" Her mother had been gone for fifteen years now and sometimes Ella wished for her too, but not nearly as often as she once had. "You're doing okay." She crossed the room to stand in front of him, touched him gently on the forearm – a little reminder that she was still here, living and breathing. They both were. "We're both doing okay. Aren't we?"

"Yes." He cleared his throat and covered her hand with the warmth of his own, patting it once, twice, and then that was enough when it came to Samuel T. and rampant displays of affection. "I should send you to Dallas. *Make* you go and live amongst people your own age."

"But I *have* lived in Dallas. For a year. In a little concrete box of a dorm room." Ella shuddered. "Dallas got old fast."

"Or I could put a personal ad in the paper for you," he grumbled. "Lapdog wanted for headstrong cattlewoman of marriageable age."

"I do like lapdogs." Ella nodded encouragingly. "Not that I've ever had one. And let's face it, Max wouldn't have made a very good lapdog at all. He'd have been opinionated and commanding, and eventually he'd have wanted to run this place." And then all the other places they owned, given that Emerson Holdings consisted of not one ranch but three, along with a sizeable livestock transport business. "That's *my* destiny."

Her father groaned. "I miss her so, *so* much."

"I know you do." Ella reached up and put her arm around her father's shoulder. He was a good, strong man and a fair boss, and she loved him to bits. He just had a thing about wanting to see her married.

Ella had nothing against the notion, but she knew what she wanted in a partner and it was a hard combination to find. A man as strong and as capable as her father. A man who was driven. A man who had pride. *A man who had no interest whatsoever in running Emerson Holdings...* and therein lay the crux of the problem. If Ella was the one running the ranch, what else was there here for such a capable man to do? "I know you want me to find someone, and I want to, I do. And he'll fit me and Emerson Holdings to perfection, you'll see. Just let me do it my way."

"Your way's not working."

Stubborn old goat, but she hugged him again anyway. "Neither's yours."

ELLA HADN'T TAKEN her father's words to heart but she didn't dismiss them either. It wouldn't hurt her to be a bit more sociable, catch up with friends. Marietta had a population of ten thousand fine souls and saw its fair share of tourists. It wasn't exactly a thriving metropolis, nestled as it was beneath soaring mountains and surrounded by valleys and rich grazing land, but it wasn't a two-bit town either. There were places to go if someone wanted to kick back and relax. Grey's Saloon gave good food and music and whatever beverage a heart desired. Or there was the newly refurbished Graff Hotel with its fancy restaurant and bar. She'd mentioned both options to her father when she'd told him she was heading out for the evening with her old school friend Joanna Talbot. Her father had liked the idea of Ella strolling around the Graff Hotel – preferably in a ball gown.

Which was undoubtedly why, come Friday night, Ella

and Jo ended up dressed in jeans and thick winter coats as they headed for Grey's Saloon instead.

"Grey's is good." Jo was a bubbly brunette who'd left Marietta to study pre-med in California, and returned two years later with remedial massage and acupuncture diplomas in hand. Word of mouth and Jo's capable touch had turned those qualifications into a thriving business. "There's a new bartender filling in for Josh. He's Australian – you should hear him speak."

"Accents are good."

"It's not just the accent, it's the voice as well. All smooth and low, with a big fat rumble of just-try-me running straight through it."

"You *are* smitten."

"Me and every other woman in Marietta, regardless of age, creed, or marital status."

"No one's that hot."

"No, but he's a really good start."

"Is he married?"

"No."

"I want to walk in and be wildly attracted to him," said Ella. "I want to be a believer."

"That's the spirit. Is Samuel T. still throwing second-born sons of wealthy ranchers at you?"

"Yep."

"Anyone interesting?"

"Nope."

"You know, you could direct some of them my way. I could find a real soft spot for the second-born son of a wealthy rancher. Even a third-born son. You should organize a party out at your place. A midsummer night's ball."

"*Me?* Organize a ball?"

"Why not? You organize everything else. Your father would be ecstatic and so would I. Remember me? Your poor single friend?"

"No balls. The Graff Hotel is having a ball. Go to that."

"I *am* going to that. And so are you."

"We're having a barn dance in April, if that helps any? My father offered the ranch as the venue the other day and the chamber of commerce took him up on it. It's promo for a big wedding giveaway competition. Apparently Marietta's going into the destination wedding trade."

"But that's wonderful! Entertainment on our doorstep. *Brides* on our doorstep, brightening our day. I may need to invent a bridal relaxation massage package."

"You should."

"Tell me you're inviting me for a sleepover on the night of the dance."

"You're invited for a sleepover the night of the dance."

"I *knew* we were friends for a reason."

They'd reached the doors of the saloon. Jo moved forward and pushed her way inside. Soft wafts of warm air met them first. Then the mellow twang of well-played acoustic guitar drifted over them. Ella looked toward the scarred wooden bar to the bartender behind it, but it was only Reese Kendrick, the saloon manager. Reese was gorgeous, no question, but he was a hard man to know, and an intimidating man, period. The only woman to ever undo Reese had been Loreli Grey... and Loreli was long gone.

A waitress headed their way. Ella knew her too. Mardie Griffin had been two years ahead of her in school and effortlessly popular, but all that had fallen away when she'd met a man who'd led with pretty words and followed up with his fists. Mardie had divorced him eighteen months into the marriage, and these days worked her butt off at Grey's to keep herself and her one-year-old daughter fed.

Mardie greeted them with a cheerful smile. "Ladies. Table for two?"

"Booth, if you can swing it," said Jo.

"I can swing it."

"Sawyer working tonight?" Jo asked next.

"Not you too." Mardie's voice was dry, very dry.

"Ella Grace wants a look. She's hoping he'll spark a little something deep down inside. I'm hoping to say I told you so."

Mardie laughed. "He's not exactly docile. And I don't think marriage is on his agenda."

"It's not on mine either," offered Ella.

Mardie slid her a puzzled glance. "So what was with the ad? Not that it wasn't awesome, because it was."

Ella blinked in confusion, and then shrugged it off.

Maybe Mardie was talking about some television commercial. Given that Ella rarely watched television at all, it stood to reason that she had no idea what the other woman was talking about.

They were halfway to the booth when Ella realized that something other was going on. Lots of eyes in this here saloon for it was Friday night and a snowy, wintery one at that. Lots of eyes fixed on her. A pair of women laughed suddenly, over by the bulletin board. Reese Kendrick looked her way and there was a warning for her in his dark, dangerous gaze... and what the hell was that for? Ella had done nothing to fan his ire of late. That she knew of. "Am I missing something?" she asked warily.

"The ad," Mardie answered, equally wary now. "*Your* ad. In the classifieds."

Ella shook her head. "I never put any ad in the classifieds."

"Go Ella!" A wolf howl followed, and Ella had no idea what that meant either.

"Mardie, I'm lost."

"How about you settle in that booth right there and I'll bring you the paper."

"Yes, but what's that got to do with anythi—"

Mardie slipped away fast and Ella walked to the booth on suddenly wooden legs. She eased into the bench seat and frowned when Jo took the seat opposite. "Do *you* know what she's talking about?"

Jo shook her head.

"I have a really bad feeling about this." It was that sinking sensation, the one she only got when she'd screwed up but good.

And then Mardie was back, drinks tray in hand and the local newspaper tucked under one arm. "Here you go, ladies. Two grapefruit daiquiris on me. Ella, yours is a double 'cause you're going to need it." Mardie set the pretty yellowy-orange colored cocktails down in front of them. The paper got slapped down on the table next. It was open at the personal classifieds.

Someone had drawn a fat red circle around one of the ads. Within the fat circle was a photograph of Ella.

"But I didn't *put* any ad in the classifieds," Ella protested, and then memory kicked in…

Lapdogs.

Her increasingly frustrated father, when it came to Ella settling down and giving him grandchildren.

Oh, *no.*

Ella whimpered, there was no other word for it. She'd become a whimpering woman.

"Would someone please tell me what's going on?" demanded Jo.

"I may have annoyed my father the other night," Ella offered jaggedly. "More than I thought. A lot. He's been threatening to send me to Dallas. I refused to go, and then there was talk about putting an ad in the paper. I didn't think he'd *do* it."

"An ad for what?" asked Jo.

Ella couldn't bear to look.

Mardie sent her a sympathetic glance. "Apparently Ella's after a docile house-husband."

Jo snatched for the Copper Mountain Courier at the same time Ella did. Ella got there first and wore Jo's slender body slamming up against her side a heartbeat later.

"Oh, look," Jo said helpfully. "A picture of you. And it's a good one."

"Color too," Mardie pointed out. "Only colored ad on the page. Makes it *pop*."

"Make it *stop*," muttered Ella as Mardie hastened away, trying to disguise her smile.

The heading on the ad was arresting.

DOCILE HOUSE HUSBAND WANTED

They read in silence. Moments later, Jo's hand crept up to cover her mouth.

"If you laugh—" Ella threatened darkly. At which point her sweet and ever loving childhood companion did a mighty fine impression of someone about to cough up a cow.

It was a full one minute and thirty-seven seconds before Jo could even speak. "I'm not laughing. I was choking."

"Have you read down further?"

Jo nodded vigorously. "I particularly like the bit about him needing to be able to cook, clean, iron, keep a tidy house, and raise well-mannered, obedient children."

"And the rest?"

"Well, who wouldn't want a man who's committed to due diligence, the greater good, and sparkling silverware?"

Ella drained her drink in one long swallow and signaled for another. "I'm going to kill him."

"Shush. If you tell everyone about it beforehand, you're not going to be able to claim temporary insanity. What do you think *excellent remuneration package* means?"

"It means I'm going to kill him."

Another grapefruit daiquiri got plonked down on the table in front of her. They must have had it waiting. "It's still on the house," drawled Mardie. "Reese says don't do anything stupid. Me, I figured you might want to know that some bright spark pinned the ad to the bulletin board too. You want me to take it down?"

"I want a piece of paper," Ella grated.

"Better than a gun," Jo said and Mardie nodded her agreement.

By the time Mardie returned with a writing pad with the saloon's logo scrawled across the top, Ella's temper had settled to a slow seethe and she had her chin up and her mortification almost under control.

"You ready to order?" Mardie asked. "Not that I'm rushing you."

"Give us another few minutes." The title would need to be eye-catching. Large print.

PERFECT LOVER WANTED

"Oh, yay," said Mardie and was gone again before Ella could gift her with a glare.

Instead, Ella underlined her heading and started in on the specific skill set required.

"Experienced, attentive, innovative—

"Male," Jo added. "You'd better put down male."

"Experienced attentive innovative *male* bedmate required for hardworking cattle dynasty heiress with no time to meet a man and no desire for a husband of any kind, docile or otherwise. Should I ask for references?"

"Yes."

"References required. Ability to alienate meddlesome father essential."

"You need to ask for a photo and a phone number as well. I know how this works."

Ella dutifully wrote "Attach photo and contact details below."

"Please," said Jo. "*Please* attach photo and contact details below. You don't want to come across as demanding."

Ella dutifully added please to the front of the sentence. "It still sounds demanding."

Jo's lips twitched. "How odd."

Ella ignored her and signed her name with a flourish. "There. All done."

"Good. Now burn it."

"No."

"Ella Grace, I know what you're thinking, and as your dear childhood friend it is my *duty* to—Ella!" Jo's voice was rising, the further away Ella got from the table. Ella was halfway to the bulletin board, her shoulders back and her gaze firmly fixed on her destination when Jo spoke again. "Ella, this is a really bad idea."

"No, I'm really liking it."

"You won't in the morning."

"My future won't look so hot in the morning anyway, what with me murdering my father and being a wanted fugitive and all. I've decided to live in the now." Ella reached the saloon's bulletin board, glared at the offending personal ad, and briskly cleared a space next to it. She stole two pins from the school band's flyer and another pin from a postcard advertising the local library, and stuck her own ad up on the board. If Samuel T. Emerson wanted to make her private life public then, dammit, she'd make it public.

She studied the ad, tilted her head to one side. Something was missing. Ella uncapped the pen and wrote MUST HAVE SPARK across the bottom in big bold capitals. Might as well live in hope.

"Jo, have you ordered yet?" Ella wasn't quite yelling. Jo wasn't quite doubled down on the bench seat trying to stifle her giggles. Reese wasn't quite ready to throw them out. Yet.

"Not, but I'm having the beef and the potato bake."

Ella smiled brightly. "Hey Mardie, we're ready to order. I'll have the trout."

SAWYER PUSHED THROUGH the swinging doors that fed from the storeroom out to the run of Grey's long bar. One of the beer taps had been spluttering like a fuel-starved engine and he'd had to go and tap a new keg. The saloon had been quiet enough when he'd left, but it was buzzing now and for no discernable reason that he could fathom.

"What's up?" he asked Mardie as she swung by with a round of empties for him.

"Remember that personal ad in this morning's paper? The one for the docile house husband?"

"Hard to forget."

"Ella Grace didn't put that ad in the paper after all. Her daddy put it in on her behalf."

Sawyer didn't know much about father-daughter relationships, but he sure as hell recognized public embarrassment when he saw it. "Father of the year."

"Ella's just written her own ad and stuck it up on the board next to the other one. She's after a lover. One who can annoy the living bejeezus out of her father."

Sawyer smiled. He liked the defiance inherent in Ella's actions. It tugged at heartstrings buried deep in his past. He knew how it felt to pull up short of parental expectations. Sawyer glanced over the customers again. "Which one's Ella?"

"Booth eight. The smaller brunette."

Sawyer looked over toward the booth. Aha. *That* brunette. He'd seen her come in, along with her friend. She wasn't all that big and she wasn't all that curvy now that she'd shed her winter coat, but there was something about her that drew the eye and held it. Her confidence, maybe. Or perhaps it was just the liveliness in her eyes. He always had been a sucker for bright eyed women, no matter the actual eye color.

Hers, he noted, were the vivid blue of cornflowers on a sunny summer's day.

"You should go read Ella's *other* ad." Mardie fished in her apron pocket and came up with a phone that she held up at eye level and pointed his way. "Let me take a photo of you first, 'cause you might want to answer it. C'mon Sawyer, *use* those dimples, look naughty–not *that* naughty, and… wow. You're really photogenic, aren't you?" Mardie's smile came at him sunny side up and full of mischief. "Hold the fort for me, lover boy. I'm just going to run this through the printer."

"Yeah, no, Mardie, I don't much like having my photo up on any walls. Got a thing about avoiding the limelight. And the wrath of *Reese*." And the press.

Then again, maybe it wouldn't hurt.

Sawyer thought back to the ridiculous personal in the paper that morning and couldn't help but laugh.

"THERE. BEHIND THE bar. Look," said Jo, and Ella looked

and then forgot what she was talking about in favor of looking some more, because he was hot, smoking hot, and he was heading out from behind the bar and striding toward the bulletin board with a sheet of white paper in hand.

His shoulders were broad and his face was a collection of strong planes and angles, no softness anywhere, and then he stopped at the board and read the ad and his eyes crinkled as he smiled, and there – right then and there – Ella felt the world around her slip a little sideways.

"Any spark yet?" Jo wanted to know. "Because *that* is Sawyer."

"Could be the two daiquiris," Ella muttered as she dragged her gaze away from him and reached for the water jug on the table. "Phew. Is it hot in here? It's hot in here."

"I knew you wouldn't be immune."

"Let's not be hasty." Ella took a quick sip of water but she couldn't quite keep her gaze away from the masterpiece that was Sawyer. "Good grief, look at those shoulders. They're almost as wide as your average door. Must make life difficult – always having to sidle in sideways."

"I thought you said you wanted to be a believer."

"I do. I do want to be a believer. How do I make him speak?"

"I hear the usual approach is to say hello." Ella and Jo watched in silence as Sawyer pinned a bit of paper below her ad. Looked like a photo. And a phone number.

"Could be he's pinning up someone else's reply," Ella

said. "No need to be all… hopeful."

Except that Sawyer turned and looked straight at her and his eyes were green, honest-to-God, no-other-color-involved, deep forest green. He quirked his lips and showed off a dimple in his cheek, and then he turned and sauntered back to the bar, easy as you please.

"I think I'm in lust," Ella wheezed. "After all these years, it's finally happened. I feel like I've just been hit by an eighteen-wheeler. What do I do?"

"Are you going to listen to my advice this time?" Jo looked skeptical. Ella nodded frantically.

"Breathe."

Chapter Two

"YOU CAN BUY her a glass of water," Reese told the loser at the bar flatly. "With ice and lime." Reese Kendrick wasn't big on words but he *was* big on maintaining order in the bar. Sawyer liked that about him; liked that Reese's fearsome reputation was usually enough to shut down trouble before it began.

Trouble was, those warring ads on the bulletin board had taken on a life of their own. Sawyer might have been the first to pin up his picture but he hadn't been the last. The ad for the perfect lover now had three more responses beneath his own, and the ad for a docile house-husband had two.

One of the house-husband contenders had sent dessert over to Ella's table instead of a drink. And she'd eaten it. Well, strictly speaking, Ella's friend had eaten most of it, but Sawyer still figured it for a nice play.

Bets were going down all across the saloon as to what the delectable Ella Grace was going to do next. Meanwhile, the number of beverages being sent her way was hitting double digits, hence Reese's decision to cut her off.

Reese sent the loser away with a glass of sparkling water.

Reese was currently eyeing *him* with the flat bleak gaze of a man lining up a sniper shot.

"What?" Some kind of defense was clearly needed. "I was *helping* when I answered that ad. What if she'd had no takers? That would have been really embarrassing."

"You're such a sweetheart," said Mardie from the other side of the bar, and then went and spoiled her defense of him with a snicker.

"Ouch. Who babysat your daughter the other day when you had to go to Livingstone?" He pointed to his chest. "Me. The sweetheart."

"I already thanked you for that, even though Mrs. Burrows saw you out walking Claire and now thinks I'm a twice fallen woman with a weakness for truck-stop trash."

"Your baby was screaming because she was bored. I defend my right to walk her around the block. We picked up fallen tree branches and Claire tried to eat them. Happiness ensued."

"You let my baby eat trees?"

"No, I let her *try*."

"Trees aside, you *do* know that the father you've pledged to help annoy is Samuel T. Emerson, of Emerson Holdings?" Reese told him dryly. "Ring any bells? Because you're living in one of his bunkhouses."

Sawyer probably should have made that connection himself; what with the Emerson name being plastered all over the transport trucks, not to mention the trucking company signage itself. "Gotta hand it to old Samuel T. He does provide good sleepover accommodation for his drivers. Clean room, good shower pressure. Really good mattress."

"You don't care who he is, do you?" said Reese.

Sawyer smiled. So did Reese.

"All this rebel bonding," Mardie grumbled. "Sawyer, how *did* you manage to rent that room at Emerson's Transport?"

"I asked. Man called Ray gave me the option of rooming by the week, cash in hand."

"You're not even on the books," Mardie told him bluntly.

Sawyer slid the last of Mardie's drinks order onto the tray. "Don't have to be if I can be out of there in ten minutes."

"Did you come by that drifter mentality the hard way, or were you just born to it?" she sniped, and Sawyer thought that maybe, just maybe, he didn't deserve that and that her comment was mostly meant for someone else. From all accounts, Mardie's ex had been a drifter too, and that probably wasn't the half of it. Sawyer had come up behind Mardie on his first day working the bar – she'd been trying to reach for a fresh bottle of top shelf whisky, and he'd watched her flinch hard then go utterly rigid when she'd realized he'd hemmed her in. He'd stepped back slowly, giving her space, lots of space, and almost let her reaction pass.

Almost.

"Okay, so next time we do that, how about you stand over there and tell me what you want down from the shelf and I'll get it for you?" he'd offered carefully, and watched some of the stiffness ease from her thin shoulders.

"Deal," she'd said in a low, ragged voice, not even turning to look him in the eye.

He hadn't asked questions. Hadn't really needed to.

They'd come to an understanding since then, and these days she trusted him enough that she could ask him to babysit her kid for a couple of hours while she went and had some x-rays taken. These days he understood her well enough that he could brush off some of her more cutting comments about his drifter lifestyle.

Most of the time.

He moved down the bar. Mardie stopped him with quiet words. "I'm sorry, Sawyer. That comment was uncalled for. It wasn't meant for you."

"We're good," he told her gruffly, for the echoes of a battered woman were all around her. "I do drift. I'm not a stable influence." And this conversation was cutting way too close to the bone and it was time he found a way out of it. "Mind you, I like to think I have a *few* useful qualities. Skills, even."

"Yeah, running your mouth," muttered Reese.

"Your customers love my mouth."

"And his eyes." Mardie was already turning away with

the loaded tray of drinks, her smile firmly back in place. "His dimples. His muscles. His ass. His utter lack of humility…"

"Find out what the odds of me landing the perfect lover position are," he called after her. "See if you can raise them. I'm just warming up."

"I'm glad to hear it," said a new voice, a feminine voice, mellow and assured. "Because for a former frontrunner, you're slipping behind. You haven't even bought me a drink."

"That's because you're cut off." Sawyer turned and there she was, all creamy skinned and restless, and even prettier up close than she had been from afar. He met her gaze and felt the force of it, the singular focus of it, and he was glad he hadn't still been talking when he turned her way because he might not have been able to finish his sentence. Some people kept their energy contained. This woman didn't seem to live by that particular philosophy at all. Instead, she exuded a vibrant energy and the air around her seemed to shimmer beneath its impact.

That, or he was getting dizzy.

He took a moment, remembered to breathe, and then smiled his best lazy smile. "I was thinking flowers for you instead of a drink."

"At this time of night? Where would you get them?"

"There's some out back in a vase. I'm not sure who they belong to but I doubt they'll be missed."

"*Stolen* flowers," she murmured. "Tell me, do they smell

sweeter?"

"They do." He let some rumble enter his voice. He'd wooed women before; he knew what worked for them. And for him.

"My father's going to love you," she murmured.

"Trust me, he won't. Although seeing as that's the point, I'd say we're good to go."

"I'm going to need some references."

Damn but she had a pretty mouth. Generously proportioned. Soft and supple looking. "I never kiss and tell."

"Convenient."

"Discreet."

"I'm really not after discreet," she told him politely. "I'm looking for a noisy, attention-getting affair with a man my father will find thoroughly unsuitable."

"For you I could be indiscreet." She leaned forward. It seemed only polite that Sawyer lean forward too.

"May I make a confession?"

"I'm all ears." Her eyes really were the most amazing shade of blue.

"It doesn't even have to be a real affair. It could be a pretend one."

From somewhere beside him, Reese snorted. Ella Grace Emerson swayed back and eyed Reese reproachfully. "You cut me off."

"I know."

"I've had two. Right at the start of the evening."

"Considering the first one was a double, that makes three. And you're still cut off. Ella Grace, I don't care who started this debacle, you or Samuel T. I do know that you're asking for the kind of trouble that isn't welcome here. So unless you want to wake up tomorrow morning naked in some joker's bed, with a splitting headache and no notion of how you got there, I suggest you take control of what you've started and change the way some people are thinking. Two choices, Ella Grace. Either you shut this down…" Reese's voice had hardened. "Or I will."

"Do you really think that's where those ads are sending us?" she asked skeptically.

"You never can tell."

"Give me your pen," she said, and Reese handed her a fat black marker with an air of quiet warning.

Sawyer watched as she stalked over to the bulletin board and crossed out the docile house husband ad completely. A groan went up from two of the tables, but it was friendly still, there was laughter still. Reese might have a sixth sense for trouble, but it wasn't upon them just yet.

Ella Grace turned and held up her hand for attention.

As if she didn't command the room already.

"Sorry," she said. "Really not after a husband. It was a joke. Carey and Ry, I'm flattered and truly grateful that you decided to play along. I've every confidence that you'll make fine husbands one day. *Really* fine if you plan on using that ad as your guide."

Ladies cheered. Carey blushed. Ry stood and raised both arms in victory. And then Ella's hand was back in the air again.

"As for the lover wanted ad, it's been pointed out to me that I may need to put a little more thought into that as well before, uh, taking action. So that notice is coming down too." Groans this time, and more laughter, all still on the bright side of sociable. "I do apologize for the misdirection, people, but I hope there's no harm done. And, um, for everyone involved, this round's on me."

"I like her," Sawyer murmured.

Reese gave him a flat stare.

"What? She did exactly what you asked her to do and she did it with style. Tell me you didn't admire that."

"She'd have impressed me more if she'd never started it."

"Well, yeah, but where's the fun in that?"

"I'm surrounded by children," Reece said, but he gave Ella a nod when she returned to the barstool. Ella's girlfriend joined her moments later, grinning hard.

"There we go," Ella said briskly, with the air of someone dusting her hands. "No one wants to marry me, no one wants to take me home and showcase their sexual prowess, and Sawyer here thinks I'm a lunatic. My work here is done."

"I love your life," said her friend. "It's big. It's got balls. What are we doing for an encore?"

"I don't know about you but I'm spent. Possibly broke.

And for some strange reason I'm also cut off from the alcoholic beverages. Want to go to your place, watch bad action movies and eat s'mores? I can put the round I just offered people on my account." Ella shot Reese an enquiring glance. "Do I have an account here?"

"You do now."

"My father will be so pleased."

She was such an autocrat, decided Sawyer. It helped that she also had a fine sense of the ridiculous. And, y'know, bright blue eyes.

She looked at him curiously, as if she couldn't quite figure out what to make of him. He quirked a brow and she seemed to come to some sort of decision. "Would you like to have lunch with me tomorrow?"

"Are you still on about the pretend lover thing?"

"Yes." Ella ran a hand though her tousled dark tresses. "No."

"Which is it?"

"Okay, maybe I *do* want my father to realize that he can't control my love life the way he controls the breeding habits of our cows, but I don't necessarily plan to use you to make him see the light. That would be unfair of me. I just figured, okay, maybe he's right and I do need to get out more and expand my social circle. It wouldn't hurt to do *that*. Besides, it's only lunch. It's no big deal. A little company. And forget what I just said about cows – you don't need to know their breeding habits, or mine. I'm just…"

"Babbling?" he offered helpfully.

"I know." She sighed. "I never babble."

He'd been here three weeks and two days, he'd been hit on half-a-dozen times a night and never once had he taken anyone up on their offer. He didn't share his bed with strangers. Didn't start things he wouldn't be around to finish. But this woman... Ella... he could stand to know a little more. "What time for lunch?"

"Noon."

Ella's girlfriend nudged Ella hard. "Ella, play nice and preserve his ego. Try and make it sound like a question."

"Oh. Right." Ella nodded and tried again. "Noon?"

It was no less a command than the first time she'd said it.

Reese coughed – probably to hide his amusement.

Sawyer smiled, sweet and slow, not bothering to hide his. He liked this woman. His body thought she was hotter than the sun and his brain wanted to know just how long she could keep a man on his toes. "All right, princess. I'll see you tomorrow at noon. Look for me by the frozen fountain in Bramble Park."

Chapter Three

SAWYER WOKE TO the knowledge that he had a lunch date with a woman with cornflower blue eyes and a way about her that had engaged every bone in his body. How long had it been since a woman had caught and held his attention like that? Not since Zoey, and he'd been barely twenty-four back then. Too young to know the trouble he was bringing down on her in the shape of his family, and too powerless to stop it from happening.

Zoey had been the only child of a wealthy father too. A Spanish princess rather than a Montana born one.

Apparently he had a type.

Loud thumping on the door interrupted his not-so-pleasant reverie. That. That was the sound that had woken him.

He could sleep through the sound of trucks coming and going, and the shouts that went with linking up the rigs, because those noises didn't concern him. This noise, on the other hand, did. He muttered a response that might have sounded like "Coming", or it might have had a suggestion as to where the noisy thumping person could go. He hauled up, wrenched open the door and stood there blinking into the sun, belatedly grateful that his low-slung PJ bottoms were on his body rather than on the floor.

Ray the truck yard foreman stood there, fidgeting. Ray knew the hours he kept, knew he'd be asleep. Ray wouldn't have woken him for nothing.

"Ray."

"Boss wants to see you."

"Whose boss?"

"Mine. His daughter didn't come home last night. Seems Samuel T. heard you might have something to do with that."

"She's not here."

"Good."

"Good gossip grapevine though. Speedy. I think she went to her girlfriend's place for cookies and pillow fights."

"He'll see you in five minutes."

Ray backed away, message delivered. Sawyer didn't bother shutting the door, he just rifled through his carryall for jeans and a clean T-shirt, dressed fast, splashed his face with water, and ran wet hands through his hair. He brushed his teeth. He had a couple of day's growth on his face but he didn't have time to shave. He reached for his coat and an apple on the way out the door.

He did have time to eat.

Samuel T. Emerson was a good looking man, with eyes almost as blue as his daughter's. He wore the same sort of well-worn work clothes as his employees, something that lifted him a notch in Sawyer's estimation. Sawyer's own father wouldn't be caught dead wearing anything but a hand-tailored suit.

"So you're Sawyer," the older man said, and Sawyer nodded and examined the skin on his apple. It had been a long time since he'd offered up a yessir. "And you met my daughter last night."

Another nod as Sawyer bit into the apple and chewed thoughtfully, and then swallowed before answering. Manners and all that. "I'm meeting her again for lunch today."

"Are you buying or is she?"

Sawyer smiled, slick and fast. "How 'bout I get back to you on that?"

The older man eyed him coldly but Sawyer remained unperturbed. He'd grown up with colder stares than this one. Meaner ones. He took another bite of his apple. And chewed.

"I know about the ad my daughter put up on the saloon bulletin board. I know how contrary she can be."

Again, Sawyer took his time chewing and swallowing before answering. "Something you might have considered when writing *your* ad."

"Perhaps." Samuel T. smiled mirthlessly. "What brings you to Marietta, son?"

"The road, mostly. Work I like. Real pretty little town."

"Are you looking for more work, Mr. Sawyer?"

He could have told the older man that he only had three more weeks left at the bar before Reese's regular bartender returned from his break, but in Sawyer's experience handing over that kind of ammunition never ended well. "Why? You got any?"

"What can you do?"

"Jack of all trades."

"Do you have an education?"

"Ivy League, can't you tell?"

Ray snorted. Sawyer smiled and continued to eat his breakfast. Happens he did have a Harvard education, courtesy of his mother's American connections and his family's abundance of money. His father had wanted him to have a business degree so that's what he'd enrolled for. His father had once been of a mind to position Sawyer somewhere within the family's extensive brewery holdings. Right up until his older brother had stopped that line of thinking dead. "I may know a little something about the liquor business," he offered. "Running a bar and the like."

"Grey's already has a manager. A good one."

"Noticed that."

Samuel T. looked him over again, with eyes that missed nothing. "Do you know cattle?"

"I know what they look like." Sawyer sighed. "Samuel, can we cut to the part where you tell me the bunk room is no longer available and you try to run me out of town?"

"What makes you think I'm going to do that?"

"You're here."

Samuel snorted. "Son, I know my daughter. Last thing I'm going to do is run you out of town, even if I could. She can get real ornery if you take her toys away."

"That a warning that your daughter's a spoiled princess?"

"Well it should be. She has a good heart though, and there's nothing I'd like more than to see her in love and happily settled."

"Hey, woah! I answered the *other* ad."

"So you did." Samuel reached for his hat. "Pay for lunch, Sawyer. Get to know my daughter, if that's what you both want. Court her if you've a mind to. I'll give any man a chance to earn my respect and hers – even a casual worker living out of one of my bunkhouses." He put his hat on and fixed Sawyer with a steady gaze. "Just don't play my daughter for her money, because that won't end well for anyone."

"I'm not that money driven."

"Maybe you're after permanent residency."

"Australian father, American mother." Sawyer studied his apple core, decided he'd had enough and tossed it in the freshly emptied office bin. "I'm already a citizen."

Samuel stared at him long and hard. Sawyer stared back.

"Are we done?" Sawyer asked with the quiet menace he usually reserved for unruly bar patrons.

Finally the older man nodded, as if he'd made some kind of decision. "There's a new brewery opened up on the outskirts of town. It's owned by a Texas oil man, name of

Jasper Flint. Maybe you should talk to him about a job if you've a mind to stick around this real pretty little town."

Samuel left Sawyer and Ray standing in the little container-built office as he headed down the steps and off toward a huge livestock transport rig already loaded with cattle. Seemed like the old man was going to deliver some cattle himself. Moments later the engine rumbled to life and Samuel T. turned the truck toward the exit gates.

"He give every man a chance to prove his worth?" he asked, and Ray nodded.

"What happens if you fail him?"

"It's your loss."

ELLA DIDN'T USUALLY spend Saturday mornings at the park on the outskirts of Marietta's town center. There was winter feeding to attend to, along with the unloading of stock and getting them drenched and immunized while they were still in the yards. Extra hands were always welcome. That was where Ella should be, where she wanted to be, because it was safe and familiar and she could be herself.

Ella wasn't entirely sure what she was doing here, or what had come over her last night when she'd asked Sawyer out to lunch. In the light of a cold winter morning it really didn't seem like such a good idea.

But an Emerson didn't go back on her word or renege on her invitations, and Bramble Park did look lovely draped in winter white. The baby snowplows had been through the grounds already, clearing the paths and running a wide circle around the frozen water fountain. A bunch of kids pelted snowballs at one another over in the direction of the courthouse, using tree trunks for cover.

Sawyer wasn't anywhere to be seen. Ella was only a couple of minutes early, but still…

Maybe he wouldn't show.

She stamped her feet to ward off the cold and then figured that she should probably stop with the stomping in case Sawyer took it as a sign of impatience. She wondered what time his bartending shift had finished. Maybe 1:30 am? Although if he stayed on through clean up… 2:00 am? Would he shower when he got home? What time would he have woken up this morning?

Maybe he wouldn't show.

Ella shoved her mittened hands beneath her armpits and figured she'd give him another five minutes before leaving. Probably better if he didn't show. That way he could remain a fantasy for years.

And then Ella turned around and there he was, all rugged up against the cold and heading toward her along one of the snow-bitten pathways and lord but he was big – it was the shoulders that made him seem so, had to be, because his legs – currently encased in faded denim – were just normal. Okay, maybe the legs were somewhat lengthier than normal. Okay, nothing about him was normal and everything was superb – may as well admit that now and be done with it.

Ella had wondered if she'd been imagining the deep kick of lust in her belly she'd felt when she first set eyes on Sawyer last night.

She'd wondered if the lust had been a fleeting thing.

Nope.

"How much do you know about cattle, Sawyer?" she asked when he reached her. He was dressed for winter – as she was. Thick coat and gloves, waterproof boots with thick grip rubber soles. Winter gear tended to swamp Ella. It didn't swamp him.

"You're the second person to ask me that today. Why do you ask?"

"I wondered if you were one of those rugged Australian Snowy Mountain men."

He grinned at her. "No."

Shame. "So how did you get your, um—" she waved her hand in his general direction. "—physique?"

"Hard labor and genetics. Hey, I bought us lunch. Well… it's either our lunch or my dinner, depending on whether you have any suggestions as to where we can eat it. I like the outdoors. Having said that, finding a picnic spot in Montana in the middle of winter with the ground under four foot of snow is a little more challenging than finding a picnic spot in Australia. I brought a picnic blanket though. Waterproof."

"You're really not from around here, are you?"

"No. Are you trying to tell me that you've never picnicked in the snow?"

"Sawyer, I have never picnicked in the snow."

"Would you like to?"

Ella studied the cloudless blue sky. It *was* a very fine winter's day.

And Sawyer had such very tempting dimples. And when he reached into the pocket of his coat and pulled out a big bag full of Sage's chocolates, Ella was sold.

"You've discovered one of Marietta's best kept secrets," she said as Sawyer tugged on the ribbon around the cellophane. "Sage Carrigan is a world-class chocolatier. Which ones did you get?"

"The salted toffee with dark chocolate swirled into it." The cellophane opened to reveal a generous supply of it.

"I'm liking this picnic a lot already," she told him, as she plucked a chocolate from his hand and popped it in her mouth.

Which finished the conversation for quite some time given that the toffee was chewy, the chocolate dribbly, and the salt crystals just made the mix perfect.

Sawyer didn't seem to mind. He just took her hand in his and stomped his way through squeaky, part-packed snow – leaving yeti tracks behind him – until he found a spot that spoke to him.

Hard to know what it said.

He withdrew a blanket from the pack on his back and

spread it out. He took off his gloves, held his hand out and helped her be seated and then sat opposite, set the chocolates in front of her and started pulling more food from his pack. A loaf of crusty bread. Crumbly cheese from the deli. Two locally made beers. Spicy avocado dip and crackers, two containers of rare-roast-beef pasta salad from Ginny's Café. Two containers of apple crumble, also from Ginny's Café – and there was another Marietta culinary experience to savor.

Ella loosened her scarf but decided against taking her woolly hat off, no matter that she'd spent an inordinate amount of time straightening her hair this morning in anticipation of having to do just that and not wanting to look a complete mess when it happened. If Sawyer wanted to picnic outside he would just have to deal with her staying bundled up.

"I'm glad I'm hungry. Are you hungry?" she asked, kneeling up and then sitting back down again, this time with her padded coat between the snow, the thin blanket and her butt.

"Yes. Do I get to eat the apple pie first?"

"I ate the chocolate first." She reached for another one of Sage's confections. "And second. Is Sawyer your first name or your last one?"

"Last."

He sounded as if he was going to leave it at that, but she gestured for him to keep going and then nudged his leg with her foot when he missed that cue.

He nudged her back but he did offer up more. "My first name's Cameron. Got a few people who call me that. My mother. A couple of aunts. A few more people call me Cam. Here in Marietta, it's just Sawyer."

"What does your father call you?"

Sawyer tensed, then deliberately reached for a takeout container full of pie and the plastic spoon that went with it. "Nothing. We haven't spoken for a while. Family rift."

"Is it mendable?"

"No."

"Do you talk to your mother?"

"On rare occasion."

"Brothers and sisters?"

"I have one brother. We don't get along. Told you I had experience when it came to alienating family." He eyed her steadily, and those eyes were even more amazingly green in the daylight than they had been at the bar. "What about you, Ella of the twenty questions? What's your background?"

"I was born here. Raised here, and sometimes raised in Texas because we have a couple of ranches there as well. I like horses, I breed arguably the best stud Angus cows in three states, and I raise fat cattle. I lost my mother to cancer when I was a kid. My father never quite got over it, or found another love. I did get over it eventually, but some of the side-effects took hold and they're a part of me now. I stick close to home because I like living in a familiar world where the people don't come and go every five minutes. I like waking up and looking out the window and knowing the mountains are always going to be there. Could be I'm slightly set in my ways. But I'm aiming to shake that up. I may even go traveling for a while."

"Where to?"

"Don't rush me."

Sawyer grinned around his spoonful of pie. Ella stripped off her gloves and reached for the beef salad and added a hefty sprinkle of Sawyer's crumbly cheese. The bread really couldn't be ignored either. Maybe she could make a roast beef salad sandwich without making too much mess.

Turns out she could.

Sawyer eyed it hungrily, so she rolled her eyes, handed it over and started making another one. "*This* one's mine."

"Never said a word."

"No, but you *looked.*"

"You're ornery."

"So I've been told. How do you do it? Travel around all the time?"

"I like seeing new faces," he told her. "New places."

"Don't you miss home?"

"No."

She studied him thoughtfully. Hard to say if he really did mean that. She didn't know him well enough to tell. "Where *is* home for you?"

He was silent a long time. "Sydney, probably. It's where I spent a lot of my childhood. But my mother's American and I have dual citizenship, so… big place, North America. Takes a while to get around it."

"Have you ever thought about settling down anywhere?"

"Once or twice."

"What stopped you?"

"Guess it wasn't what I was looking for."

Conversation lapsed as they ate haphazardly. Good sandwiches. Sweet and cold beer.

"Your father came to see me this morning," he murmured.

"How'd he know where you live? I don't even know where you live."

"I'm staying in one of the bunkrooms at Emerson's Transport."

Ella grimaced. Yep, that'd do it. "What did he want?"

"Meet and greet."

"What did he *say*?"

"Not a lot."

"C'mon Sawyer, spill. I need to know whether to berate him or not. I'm thinking yes, just on principle."

"He warned me against chasing you for your money."

"*Are* you planning to chase me for my money?"

"No."

"That's a relief. Are you planning on chasing me at all?"

"I'm not sure yet."

"You're not exactly crazy about me, are you?"

There were those dimples again. He should register them

as a lethal weapon. "Don't rush me."

She laughed because he was playful and smart and those dimples encouraged laughter. "Where'd you go to college?"

"What makes you think I did?"

"Gut instinct."

"See, if I told you, you'd put me in a different box. And I like the box I'm in."

"The international man of mystery box does have a lot going for it," she said agreeably. "Apart from making me feel downright home grown."

"They do grow many fine products around these parts."

"You said products. The minute you start talking supply and demand, I'm going to call you a marketing major."

"Did you get a tertiary education, Ella?"

"I went to University of Texas for a year. I tried business. Pulled some good grades, probably because I'd already learned a lot about business from my father. Maybe I'll go back one day and try a few more subjects but right now I've no plans in that direction."

"Because your father knows it all?"

"Because I have a really good life here and I don't want to leave it."

"So you have everything you want right here?"

"Well, my father would say I need a husband, and while I'm not wholly opposed to the idea I'm not entirely convinced that I *need* one. I could do want *and* need, I guess. Best of both worlds. And I really want to do lust, husband or not."

His eyes smiled down at her, as if he found her highly amusing. "Have you ever *been* in lust?"

"No, but I'm ever hopeful. You've no idea how long I've waited to feel the lust."

He was sitting on the picnic blanket, leaning back on his hands, pure sun-spelled, lounging male. "There's a chance I could teach you something about that." His voice had roughened. Best bedroom voice ever.

"Now is good." That wasn't too pushy, was it? She was just being accommodating.

Sawyer's gaze was very intent. "Trouble is, lust can strip your control. Make you vulnerable. Make you want to do naughty things in a public park with half a dozen people looking on. You ready for that, Ella?"

Chances were he'd just hit a kink she never knew she had, what with the tight knot of heat forming in her belly and all. "So if I were to slide on over and straddle your legs and sit in your lap and just nibble on something…"

"We might both learn something."

Ella was already moving, skirting the food, straddling his legs so that she was kneeling above him at first before sitting herself tentatively just above his knees.

"Closer," he ordered gruffly.

And…*oh!* Well.

"Better?"

"You're really, um, hard-bodied. And warm. Phew."

"We've been sitting in the sun."

Yeah, winter sun. In the snow. Minus double-digit degrees.

"Would you like to take the lead?" he murmured, his lips brushing her ear while her body went soft and pliant. "Or do you want me to do it?"

"You." Chances were she could learn something. "You lead."

With his lips he drew a lingering path from her ear to her lips, stopping at the edge of them so she could draw breath and prepare. He still leant back on his hands, leaving her a way out should she want to take it. She liked that about him. And then he lifted his knees and slid her more snugly into his lap, the smile in his eyes as cheeky as the maneuver.

"You've done this before," she accused.

"You wanted experience."

True. "What else you got?"

"This." His next move was pure, slow-motion beauty as he leaned in and brushed his lips against hers. Nothing but a tease and a torment, not even all that warm. And then his lips were on her again, opening, coaxing, and *now* they were warm, and Ella responded with a gasp and a great big need for more.

He was good at kissing, better than good, and his lips tasted like salted toffee, and his big hand was gentle as he cupped her jaw and took from her whatever the hell he had a mind to take.

A lazy taste. A hint of teeth against the curve of her lip and it was effective. So, *so* effective, and she shifted against him and gave in to the temptation to wrap her arms around his neck and slide a little deeper into the moment.

There was no park. No people who might be watching.

She'd wanted lust, wanted to know the strength of it and what it could do. She never imagined that it could make the world around her disappear.

And then his arm came around her waist and he shifted beneath her until he had her pressed hard against him, positioned just right for—

She was whimpering again. She was an undulating, whimpering woman and her body knew exactly what it wanted to do with him, even if some small fragment of her mind was trying to tell her something else.

"Not here." His voice was gruff and halfway to pleading. "Ella, pull back. Public park. Children."

"What about them? Pregnancy is very unlikely; you're not even naked yet."

"Children *in the park*." His hand slid to her neck, his thumb tracing circles behind one ear, just beneath her woolly hat. He slid it down her back in what was probably meant to be soothing fashion. Instead, she rode the rough pressure of it all the way down to her hip.

And then he tipped her sideways, tipped her onto her back and she was staring up at the sky and then at Sawyer, who'd opted to sit up and reach for the pie she hadn't yet eaten. He held it out toward her.

As if pie could compete with the taste of *him*.

She sat up and took it grudgingly.

He smiled at that. "There are a dozen people watching us. If you were wanting your father to hear about our wild display of public affection, consider it done."

"Oh." She glanced around. They had indeed attracted plenty of attention. "I'm sorry about your reputation. It's probably just been trashed."

"How so?"

"See, I've never been quite so..." Ella searched for the right word. Crazy? Reckless? *Forward?* Yeah, she didn't feel like mentioning any of those. "I've never been quite so *enthusiastic* in my approval of someone before. And you're not from around here. Chances are you'll be seen as a troublemaker, just dying to lead me astray. *Are* you dying to lead me astray?"

"I don't know about the *dying*. That's something I'd rather avoid. Are you going to eat that pie?"

"No." Sawyer's stomach was a bottomless pit, but she didn't hand him her pie. Instead, she held it firmly out of arm's reach, an action which served only to amuse him more. "Are you going to lead me astray?"

"Yes." He smiled sweet and lazy. "I do believe I'm inclined that way."

"Oh, good." Ella smiled back, bright as a daisy, and handed him the pie.

Chapter Four

THERE WAS A downside to taking up with Marietta's Ella Grace Emerson, Sawyer discovered, when he arrived for his shift at the saloon three days later. Sawyer had known they were making their date public when they'd had it in the park in full view of anyone with eyes to see. They'd met for coffee the day after that, and this morning Ella had been in Marietta getting parts for something or other so he'd met her at Ginny's Café for an early lunch. Which seemed to suggest to some people that Ella had spent the night with him.

He'd thought he'd be able to handle it, handle her.

He'd been wrong.

He tried to ignore the renewed interest in his good self and his background, but halfway into his shift Mardie was slanting him worried glances and Sawyer was damn glad that Reese wasn't around to watch him grow clipped with the customers and free with his scowl.

The fine folk of Marietta were nosy, he understood that.

They were protective, he understood that too. They wanted to know if he was good enough for their Ella Grace.

And that wasn't a question he wanted to answer.

The picnic had gone well. Sawyer liked Ella Grace Emerson, really liked her. They'd strolled through the park after lunch. He'd kissed her again, standing up this time, in the hope of better control.

Yesterday after lunch he'd ended up pinning her against a tree, the rough bark digging into his fingers as he slaked his hunger, and hers, because he hadn't been alone in his passion, oh no. Ella Grace had matched him gasp for soaring gasp.

He wanted to know what she was like first thing in the morning. He wanted to see her astride a horse. Tending her cows. He just plain *wanted*.

And then he wondered what it might be like to have Ella at his side on a more permanent basis and that scared him, that thought, because sooner or later his family would find out and his family was seriously dysfunctional, and exposing a woman to that wasn't something he ever wanted to do.

"Hey, Aussie." Mardie didn't corner him until the end of the night when she was counting cash and Sawyer was tallying up the beverages that had gone over the bar. "Want to tell me what's wrong?"

"Nothing's wrong."

"Sawyer, sweetie, you're a little more transparent than you think. You've been brooding half the night. Is it Ella? I heard about lunch."

"Everyone heard about lunch."

"So? Ella got what she wanted. You got what you wanted. Sounds like a fine time was had by all."

Sawyer shrugged. He started measuring the spill in the beer trays into a stainless steel bucket. They'd had a good night when it came to beer sales but there was more spill than usual. "How many new kegs did the boss tap tonight?"

"Three. And he swapped out the new Jimmy's Creek Blonde before it was due, because a couple of our regulars thought it tasted off."

"He tip those drinks down the sink or did they go into the spill?"

"Didn't notice."

Sawyer figured they *had* probably gone into the spill and that the trouble with the Blonde keg would account for the extra.

"Spill volumes make more sense now?" asked Mardie.

"Yeah, we're square."

"I swear, under all that lazy charm you're as thorough as Reese."

"Good to know."

Sawyer hadn't changed his name. No matter where he went, he never did that. If Reese or the bar's owner, Jason Grey, wanted to search for Cameron Sawyer on the Internet and start putting two and two together, the information would be there. Youngest son of international brewery magnate Laurence Sawyer. Youngest son of Catherine Allbright-Sawyer. Brother of Richard Sawyer, the golden child who was brewery heir and rampant psychopath…

Though maybe that last bit wasn't on the Web. Yet.

Yeah, Cameron Sawyer had a heritage and a history all right.

But it wasn't one he wanted to share.

Mardie was still frowning at him and this time he called her on it. "What? I'm good, Mardie. I'm fine."

"You really don't like talking about yourself much, do you? You don't like people getting up in your business."

"Does anyone?"

"Is that what got you so terse with people tonight?"

"Probably." Sawyer met Mardie's gaze square on. "Yes."

Mardie sighed. "You're a nice guy, Sawyer. Mind you, I'm the worst judge of men in the world."

Sawyer felt his lips hitch toward a smile. "Thanks."

"My point *being* that if you have something to hide I'm not going to pry. People are entitled to their secrets. But."

"There's always a *but*."

"*But*, if you ever did happen to fall into a sharing mood, I can personally vouch for Ella as someone who knows how to listen. Someone who can keep her mouth shut and just be there for a person. She did that for me, and we weren't best friends to begin with, if that's what you're thinking. I used to have other friends. Fair-weather friends who didn't even try to stick around when my going got ugly."

"You're not helping. I need to like Ella *less*, not more."

"Oh… well, why didn't you say so? I'm sure I can help

you there. Ella's opinionated, she doesn't tolerate fools, she can buy and sell you and chances are she's smarter than you. If she is, she'll let you know."

Sawyer grinned.

Mardie laughed. "It's not working, is it?"

"What do you mean it's not working? I'm daunted. Dismayed."

"Try saying that *without* the goofy grin on your face." Mardie shook her head. "Sawyer, my friend, when it comes to Ella Grace, you are well on your way to gone."

MAYBE MARDIE'S WORDS were meant to be playful, but after they'd finished for the night and left lock-up to the taciturn Jason Grey… after he'd seen Mardie to her car and watched her pull out onto the road… Sawyer headed walked the few blocks to the park again, rather than to his pickup.

So far he'd had three dates with Ella, though you could hardly call a stroll down Bramble Lane and a mug of hot chocolate afterwards a date. A man *couldn't* be thinking of forever after only three dates. It was too soon, way too fast. Not even on the menu. That kind of thinking was crazy in more ways than one.

His breath huffed white and his throat stung with the sub-zero air, and Sawyer hunched down into his jacket and found a bench to sit on, before pulling out his phone and looking up what time it was in Spain. Lunchtime. A good time to call. He took his time thinking about what he might say, and whether it was wise to ring at all, then he found a number and dialed it and waited. He needed to talk to someone who understood the consequences of him introducing a woman to his family. Someone who wasn't family. Preferably a woman who'd been there, done that.

He needed to talk to Zoey.

"Cameron!" She always sounded glad to hear from him, and he adored her for that. He always remembered why he'd fallen for her in the first place when she did that.

"Zoo. How's things?"

"Cameron, how many times do I have to tell you not to call me Zoo?" It was an old tease, and a hauntingly familiar reply, and he felt himself unwind just a bit because of it. "Maya's six now. And Amalie four. How did that happen? And Manuel has just bought us a summer house in Andalusia. I'm well, Cameron. We're all well. And you?"

Zoey had got married eventually, to a man who adored her. She had two little girls, dark eyed and happy. She had a good life.

He shouldn't have called.

"I'm well, Zoey." He was, wasn't he? "I'm fine."

"Cameron." Zoey had the gentlest scolding voice in the world. Effective though. "I can hear that you're not."

"I met a girl."

Zoey's silence weighed heavily on him. Sawyer stared at the snow clad trees, at the shadows cast in their wake and then at the stars in the sky, and waited while Zoey found her voice.

"You can't lock your heart away forever, my friend," she offered quietly. "You have too much to give. What's she like?"

"She's fearless, Zoey. And I never want to see that taken from her."

More silence.

"He's still there. Doing what he does." His brother. Richard Sawyer, family golden boy. Protected by family money and their father's clout. Above the law. Barely constrained by it. And driven by passion after passion, one of which was to destroy anything and everything his younger brother held dear. Zoey had been in Richard's sights once. Because Cameron had claimed her. Because Richard had wanted her.

And Zoey had paid a hefty price.

"I don't know what to do."

"Have you spoken to your mother about her?"

"No."

"She might be able to gauge things. She might be able to help."

"Did she help you?"

Zoey's silence was telling. "Your mother was blindsided," said Zoey eventually. "As were we all. Don't discount her as an ally though, Cameron. She was very kind to me. And very fond of you."

"Yet she supported Richard's behavior."

"I don't believe she did. Your mother was silenced, like the rest of us. There's a difference."

"I've had a couple of dates with her. Three." Four, if he counted the night they'd first met – which couldn't be counted as a date at all given that he'd been working. "Already I'm trying to figure out how I can make this work."

"I like her already."

"She breeds cows."

"So does Manuel. Bring her to Spain, I want to meet her. She'll be safe here with us, you know that. Richard's reach does not extend here."

"You don't know that for sure." One of the main reasons Zoey was safe now was because Sawyer was no longer in her life. A phone call once a year was one thing. Going to visit her and Manuel was a different level of involvement altogether and one he would never attempt.

"Are you still restructuring the soft drink industry up in Alaska?"

"No, I finished with that six months ago. I'm a bartender in Montana now."

"Cameron," she scolded again. "Bartending? But why?"

"Why not? I like the people. It seemed like a good idea at the time. Did I mention that I bought a house on the Washington coast just south of Seattle? The aim is to live in it more than three weeks a year."

"I like that aim. Maybe you should fill your house with a

woman to love and a family to raise. Does she know? Does this woman know who you are?"

"No."

"My friend, that is not a good start."

"I know."

"Your family will always be your family, Cameron, whether you choose to acknowledge them or not."

"I'd rather not."

"I know that. And yet…"

"How do I do it, Zoey? How do I keep her off his radar?"

"You don't. You stand your ground and you be prepared for whatever comes your way – both of you. You can't do that if she remains unaware. Tell her who you are. Tell her what you fear. It's her best protection."

But Sawyer didn't want to tell Ella who he was, didn't want to lay that filth before her. His silence said it for him.

"You said she was fearless. Let her be that for you." Zoey's voice had thickened, her accent had become more pronounced. "I wish I could have been that for you. *Te deseo amor*, Cameron. I wish you love. Always."

He closed his eyes. Wished her all the love in the world right back. Just not his. "You too, Zoey. You too."

Chapter Five

SAWYER CALLED ELLA from the chocolate shop the following lunch time. He'd been driving himself crazy with indecision all morning. A little more of her wouldn't hurt anyone, he'd think with one breath. Don't be a player, he'd scold himself with the next. And with his third breath he tossed around the notion of telling Ella who he was and the challenges he faced and letting her make her own decision.

She seemed like a woman who might appreciate not having decisions made for her.

"I need a chocolate recommendation," he began. "I ate them out of salted toffee and dark chocolate swirls."

"You want the dark-chocolate-coated ginger strips." It was noisy at her end. Windy. "Trust me, your life will never be the same again."

"What are you doing?"

"Shifting early-calving cows to a more weather-protected part of the ranch. There's more snow forecast."

"Talking to you can be very daunting."

"Does that mean you don't want to come out and see for yourself what goes on around here? Because that was my next move. I was giving you one more day to make *your* next move."

"Good of you."

"I *know.* Have I mentioned that cows with frosted eyelashes are the cutest things ever?"

"You really are a cowgirl, aren't you?"

"Born and bred. Am I tempting you?"

"Are you dusty, dirty and wearing cowboy boots and a plaid shirt?"

"I am neither dusty nor dirty. You're thinking of summer clothes or possibly Australia. Right now my hands are half frozen inside my gloves, my jeans and boots are cold and damp and my waterproof jacket isn't quite living up to its name."

"Are you at least wearing a cowboy hat and sitting astride a horse?"

"I'm sitting astride a snowmobile, greenhorn. But I do have the hat."

Sawyer took a moment to picture her as described. Then he pictured her coming apart in his arms. No telling how many times he'd pictured *that* in the past twenty-four hours. "How'd your father go with our public display of affection in the park?"

"He hasn't mentioned it. But everyone else thinks you're a dreadfully bad influence, so I'm calling it a win. If you head out here mid-afternoon we should be done with the cows, I can make an effort to be more presentable than I am now, and I can take you up into the ranges and we can get stranded in the mountain lodge overnight. Bring the ginger strips."

"And here I was going to suggest dinner and a movie."

"It's a very nice lodge. Open fireplace. Hearth rug. Food in the pantry."

"Here's the thing." He stood in the chocolate shop. Looked up and saw just how many people were listening in and decided to take this conversation outside. "The kind of privacy you're talking about isn't going to make resistance easy. We get up there and get cozy, and you *know* what's likely to happen between us. Yesterday should have made that very clear."

"It did. Am I being too forward?" She didn't wait for his reply. "I am, aren't I? I blame the lust. Come on out to the ranch, Sawyer, and take a look around. I'll take the lodge off the menu. You can put dinner on the menu. I would love to have dinner with you. Very respectable pastime."

"Do you always backtrack quite this rapidly?"

"I'm impulsive, in case you hadn't noticed. Backtracking is part of the deal. It happens every time common sense takes hold." Ella sighed heavily. "I've been sitting here waiting for a cow to get up but I don't think she can. I may have to shift the others and come back to her. What time did I say I was getting in this afternoon?"

"Mid afternoon."

"Better make it later."

"You want a hand?"

"You can tell a lot about people by the way they handle cattle," she mused. "It'll show you the man. Or the woman, as the case may be. I really hope I don't disappoint you. How soon can you get here?"

"Depends where you are."

"I keep forgetting you're not from around here. That was a compliment, by the way." She gave him directions. "Takes about fifteen – twenty minutes to get here from Marietta. Dress warm and bring a change of clothes."

Twenty minutes later, Sawyer was driving his pickup through one of the prettiest valleys he'd ever seen. Bad weather was indeed closing in on them, the sky confirmed it, but it hadn't yet arrived and the landscape sat bathed in that weirdly intense glow that photographers loved.

Ella and her father ran a beautiful operation. One where the fences glowed white, the barns were full of hay, and the ranch house itself sprawled low and loose in the foothills of a vast mountain range. Grazing cows shone glossy black and strongly muscled against the snow and every vehicle on the place was at most only a couple of years old.

Plenty of fat in Emerson's bottom line, from what Sawyer could see.

Plenty of time to figure Ella for a chip off the old block when she came into view around the side of the main barn, for she was dressed for work and her pace was brisk as she pointed to a place to park, up beside a snowmobile that had an accompanying sled loaded with hay.

He got out and reached back across the seat for his gloves and a woolly hat. "Hey."

"Just this minute loaded," she told him with a cheerful grin. "I'm aiming to get out to the cow and back before this weather hits. She's calving, which is much better news for us than her being down for reasons unknown. She's also one of our maiden heifers and she's about three weeks early… that, or she got put in the wrong group… which is why we need to take another look." Ella handed him some goggles and reached for the pair slung over the seat of the snowmobile. "You ever driven one of these things?"

"Yeah. We used them all the time in Alaska."

"What were you doing up there?"

"Restructuring a soft drink company."

Ella turned to look at him. "Who *are* you?"

"Ginger strip?" He was going to tell her. He would. He just needed to find the right time.

He pulled one out of the bag in his pocket and dangled it in front of her, and she took it and thanked him and bit into it with one hand while she straddled the snowmobile and motioned him to get on behind her. She slipped her goggles on and moments later set the machine to moving.

Ella drove with a confidence that came of long experience and a preference for speed that Sawyer enjoyed. She sped them across flat snowy grazing land and then began to climb the foothills. Not once did she let up on the gas.

Sawyer tucked his hat more firmly over his ears. Cold wind peeled across the bare sections of his face. Ella was bearing the brunt of the biting wind and she didn't complain. They crested a ridge and she slowed to a halt and pushed her goggles up but she didn't get off the snowmobile so neither did he. He pushed his goggles up too and stared out over the valley below them.

"The creek forms part of our border," she said and pointed to the thin, snaky line cutting through the valley floor. "We're also bordered by the road and the ranges." More pointing ensued. And then she pointed uphill, toward a rough track that climbed steeply. "They run a big snowmobile race across the range every year. It starts here. Occasionally I win it. People say it's because I have the home advantage across some of the course. I prefer to think that I really am just that good."

"I guess that's why you don't seem to mind when the front end of this thing lifts four feet in the air."

"That's just because we're back-heavy at the moment."

It wasn't *just* because of that. "What are you like in powder, and without the sled on the back."

"Sawyer, I am goddamn poetry in motion."

Sawyer grinned at her total lack of modesty. "Please tell me you wear a helmet."

Ella turned and flashed him a killer smile. "I do. We just

haven't put them on this time because we're going so *slow*."

Yeah, not that slow.

"What does your father think about your relationship with speed?"

"He prefers to call it my reckless disregard for safety. That answer your question?"

"Yup."

"My father had me take lessons from a national race champ a few years back – in the interests of improved safety. The extra speed was just one of those happy coincidences. The champ even offered me a place on his race team. Alas, that wasn't all he wanted and unfortunately there was no spark. I'm a little particular about that. Ask anyone."

"How 'bout I take your word for it?"

"Or you could do that." She shifted her goggles back over her eyes and got them moving again, and then turned back toward him. Sawyer immediately wanted her to turn back and watch where she was going. He pointed dead ahead, his arm bracketing hers. "What's that? Halfway up the mountain?"

"That's the lodge. You're really rather big and all-encompassing when you set your mind to it, aren't you?"

"You need more room?"

"No. Warmest I've been all day." She leaned back against him and he tucked his arm beneath hers and wrapped it around her waist. Even with all her layers of winter clothing he could still gather her close with ease.

Long time since he'd offered a woman that kind of closeness and protection.

Long time since he'd done anything but pull away. "I like your ranch," he rumbled over the whistle of the wind and the noise of the snowmobile. "It's big. It's wildly beautiful. It's well maintained."

"My father's pride and joy," she yelled back.

"Thought that was you?"

"No, I'm third in line – behind the bulls. I just get shown off a little more often than the other two because I can talk."

But Ella didn't do much talking the rest of the trip, and Sawyer was content to save his breath, enjoy the ride and the feel of Ella in his arms, and the sense of purpose that came of heading out to tend an animal that was in Ella's care.

Responsibility and ownership. How long since he'd felt the weight of that particular combination? Oh, he'd go in and take responsibility for a broken business and nine times out of ten he could turn it around, but he never took ownership. Not in the way Ella and her father had taken ownership of this place. Not in the way his own father had agonized over decisions regarding the brewery and probably still did.

They reached Ella's stranded cow a good fifteen minutes later. The cow was lying on her side, all stretched out, and Ella stifled a curse and was off the snowmobile, sinking into the snow and cursing before stomping her way to the sled and cutting the string on the bale of hay moments later.

"She won't want to eat but if you put some by her head, I'll do the back end and see if I can figure out where she's at with delivering." Ella gathered up an armful of hay, so Sawyer did the same. The cow mooed at him and tried to sit up as he tromped toward her. He tromped a little more gently so as not to frighten her more.

"Hey, girl," he murmured as she craned her neck to see what Ella was doing.

Ella, who was spreading hay out over the snow and moving in close to examine the cow's rear end and then cursing up a storm – to be specific.

"We have feet," she said when he joined her. "Hind feet instead of front feet. The calf is breech. Which does explain why mama cow is taking her time."

"What do we do?"

"Pull."

Ella stripped off her gloves and started taking off her coat. Then she took off the plaid shirt he'd teased her about on the phone, leaving just a short sleeved T-shirt and hopefully some kind of thermal wear under that. The shirt went over the seat of the snowmobile, the coat went on the ground on top of the hay and then Ella knelt on the coat and, without further comment, slid her hand over the feet of the calf and into the cow.

Her whole hand.

Then up to her elbow.

Then more until she was almost in up to her armpit.

"I hope you're not squeamish," she offered with a grimace, as she blew a strand of wayward dark hair out of her face. She followed her words with a quick gasp of pain as the cow's stomach rippled and the cow out-and-out groaned. "It's mighty squeezy in here when they start contracting."

"Uh huh." That was pretty much all he had by way of comment. Long time since he'd been lost for words.

Then again, he'd never before seen anyone use a cow as a hand puppet.

"The good news is that the calf's not that big and the front legs and head are where they need to be. Heart's still beating. You just need a bit of help, don't you, baby?"

Ella withdrew her arm slowly, to the accompaniment of more contractions. She rubbed at her wrist and took a deep breath, let it out, and reached for the two little sticking-out feet. And then she braced *her* feet against the rump of the cow, waited for the next ripple of the animal's belly and pulled, using her entire body as leverage. She gained an inch or so of back legs.

And the minute the contractions stopped, they slipped back to where they'd been before.

"Okay, then." Ella slid him an assessing glance. "So. We have a couple of options. Want to get your gloves off and join me? I'll direct, you pull, and come the next set of contractions I think we might be in business."

He took his gloves off. Took his coat off too and draped

it around Ella's shoulders. "I know you said you wanted to get down and dirty with me, but this wasn't quite what I had in mind."

"It's not exactly my first preference either, but at least I get to see those muscles of yours at work. There's a bonus right there." She made room for him and he settled down beside her on the coat atop the hay and then the snow. She put her hands on his, and they were cold and sure and ever so slightly sticky as she guided them toward the legs of the calf. "You want to get a good grip just above the hock, and instead of pulling up toward the tail, we want to pull out and down a little as the pelvis appears. Don't pull until she's pushing. Try and work with the cow."

"Got it." He had two warm and slimy little hocks in his hand and a woman at his side that he wanted more than ever. He was hopelessly out of his depth. "Work with the cow. I've never worked with a cow in my life. What does that even mean?"

Ella grinned and snugged in alongside him, sharing her warmth and part of the coat. She'd bracketed his waist with her thighs, her legs tucked up under her as she leaned in against his shoulder and set the palm of her hand between his shoulder blades. "Just have a little tug. Test the resistance. Get a feel for it."

"Have a little tug, she says. It's like my favorite fantasy ever. Minus the cow." And the hay. And the cold and the storm front coming in. And the life or death situation.

Ella ran her other hand down his forearm and rested her fingers around his. "I love this stuff. Makes me feel useful. Okay, here we go. You need to pull hard and smooth, and don't stop until I say so. 'Cause she's getting ready to push."

Push the cow did, and Sawyer took a deep breath, took a firm grip and pulled.

And then pulled that little bit harder.

"Steady," Ella murmured. "Nice and even, just a little bit more. Out and down. Yes, just like that." And then the cow kicked and shifted, and then the calf's back legs were out and then the pelvis and then the rest. One slimy, limp little calf, and Ella was moving forward, putting the palm of her hand to the baby's chest, just behind its front leg, and then that hand was moving again, pulling mucous away from the mouth and stripping it from its nose and then the calf was moving, and coughing and Ella was calling it a good girl and moving away, cleaning her hands and arm with snow, and then the hay, and then finally wiping her hands on her jeans before reaching for her shirt. "I *will* shower before dinner. I promise."

Sawyer laughed as he got to his feet in order to avoid being trampled by one very eager mama cow who was up and turning toward her calf. Moments later she was nosing and nudging and licking its little face. "What now?"

Now we wait for the calf to get to its feet and have a drink. Ella glanced at the sky, her eyes narrowing. "And then I think we might help dry the calf off and put it on the sled, and get them to shelter with the others. The cow will follow."

Ella picked up her coat and shook it out, put it on and shoved her hands into the pockets. "Brrr. Bit chilly out."

"And you do this how often?" he asked politely.

"Not that often." She looked bright eyed, rosy cheeked and utterly content. "You did well, bartender."

"What would you have done if I hadn't been here?"

"Used the calf pullers strapped to the sled. But a hand-pull has more finesse, and besides, I wanted to see what you could do. You've a strong and steady way about you, Sawyer, underneath all that charm. You made it look easy and I know for a fact that it's not. Gonna make a cowboy out of you yet."

"Let's not get carried away."

"You don't want to be a cowboy?"

"Put it this way… did you ever dress up as a kid?"

Ella nodded. "Annie Oakley, sharpshooter."

"I was the fireman."

Chapter Six

I T HAD TURNED five by the time they'd got cow and calf settled with the others, all of them protected from the worst of the incoming storm by a stand of trees and a horseshoe shaped hill. It was the most protected corner of the ranch when the weather was coming in from the south east and was a godsend when it came to winter calving.

Sawyer had followed her lead, easy as you please, when it had come to getting the calf onto the sled. He'd held the calf in place, with Ella driving and the anxious mother cow bringing up the rear. Not too fast and not too slow, with one eye on the encroaching weather and the other eye on all concerned. They unloaded the calf and the rest of the hay once they reached their destination, and Ella waited until cow and calf had settled before bumping shoulders with Sawyer to get his attention. "Now we can go."

He nodded, and she took him the fast way back to the barn, stopping only for Sawyer to open and close gates along the way. Driver drove, passenger got the gates. It was a time honored tradition – ask anyone on the land. And still…

"Am I bossy?" she asked once they were back at the barn and she'd parked the snowmobile and sled up against the western wall, just shy of the big double doors that now stood closed. Fat flakes of snow drifted down on them, not a blizzard yet, but not far off. Sawyer's pickup would get them the house with this amount of snow on the ground, no problem. Hard to say whether it'd get them to Marietta tonight though. "Did you find me bossy out there?"

Sawyer glanced her way, his gaze disconcertingly direct. "If you're talking about telling me how to pull a calf, I needed direction and you gave it. Doesn't make you bossy. It makes you strategically resourceful and me grateful."

"Strategically resourceful," she grumbled, even as his words filled her with pleasure.

"It's a compliment. Confident, capable, strategically resourceful women are incredibly hot."

"Even ones who've just had their hand up a cow?"

"It was more like your entire arm."

"Yeah." Ella sighed. "Really not the image I was hoping to present."

"Ella."

They'd reached the passenger side door of his truck. Next second he'd opened it for her, reached for her hat and tossed it inside. He smiled down at her with those crinkly eyes and the dimples and Ella couldn't help but smile back. It was a tentative smile though, maybe even anxious. She knew who she was, good traits and bad, and sometimes she wished for more subtlety and finesse, and sometimes she wished that her mother had lived long enough to teach her how to be less of a cowhand and more of a lady.

She *had* wanted Sawyer to see who she was and the world that she loved.

She'd also been hoping to break him in a little more gently.

"That memory of you with the cow is going into the memory bank alongside the one of you presiding over Grey's Saloon." He tugged his gloves off and tossed them in the truck too. "And the one of you sitting in the snow making sandwiches, and the one of you getting altogether lost in a kiss. And now I have one of you with snowflakes in your hair. It's a collage, this picture I'm building of you." He kissed her, sweet and fleeting, and then he set his lips to the spot on her cheek where a snowflake had just landed and Ella felt like melting right along with it. "And it's amazing."

"I bet you say that to all the girls." How could a few muttered words and a whisper of a kiss make her feel this gooey inside?

"No." He pulled away, his smile crooked and his eyes troubled. "I don't."

THEY REACHED THE house and Ella took him through the side entrance, straight into the mudroom where they shed their coats and boots and hats and anything else that was wet. Sure, he was a visitor, but he'd also been a cowhand for the afternoon and hopefully they were past standing on ceremony with each other. From there she took him through the huge galley kitchen, with its bank of east facing windows and from there she showed him through to the adjacent wash room; the one with the super pressure and the oversized shower head. She gave him towels and fresh soap. She may even have sighed wistfully as she'd watched him close the bathroom door behind him.

"I'm going up to another shower," she said, loud enough so that he could hear. "Help yourself to tea, coffee or whatever else you want when you come out."

"Okay."

Ella went to her room and set her own shower to scalding and then she got in and scrubbed everywhere, twice, before declaring herself squeaky clean and starting in on her after shower care. Lotion. Comb. Teeth. Towel wrapped around her while she stood in her walk-in-closet and wondered what to wear for a night out at a restaurant or a night snowed in here, the latter seeming more likely by the minute given the way the snow was coming down outside.

She stood there for a full five minutes, undecided, before stalking back out to her dresser and picking up her phone. Hopefully Sawyer had his phone on him too.

He picked up on the second ring. Guess that was a yes.

"I'm still in the bedroom, trying to decide what to wear," she told him without preamble. "And I usually don't much care what I wear. It's very odd, this desire to please you. Do you think it has something to do with the lust?"

"Everything to do with the lust," he told her dryly. "You want to hope that the level of lust fades as you get to know me better, otherwise you're going to want to please me *all the time*."

"I can see how that would get tedious, but back to the now. What shall I wear?"

"You're really task oriented, aren't you?"

"I think it's a family trait. I'm also standing here in a towel and it's getting chilly. At this point, clothes would be good."

Silence.

"Sawyer?"

"I'm trying to decide if you're torturing me deliberately."

"Rest assured, that is my intention."

"Wear whatever's comfortable, Ella." There was a smile in his voice. "Rest assured you're going to torture me anyway."

Ella grinned as she went back to her wardrobe. She narrowed her eyes and gnawed on her lower lip before finally reaching for her favorite pair of jeans. They were low slung, soft to the touch and perfectly comfortable.

Bonus points for being blue.

She had a yellow top in there somewhere, with three-quarter sleeves and a pretty sweetheart neckline. Team it with a burgundy, hot-pink and grey plaid shirt and she still looked country but not staggeringly so. Add a ring for her forefinger – a wide white-gold one – and a yellow band for her hair and she figured she looked ready for just about anything, which she was, and relaxed, which she most definitely was not.

How many times had she shown visitors around the house? Too many to count.

How many times had she fretted about what to wear while doing so?

Never ever before.

Cameron Sawyer was a bad influence. And that was before she factored in all the naughty things she wanted to do with him.

Ella found him in the kitchen, looking freshly washed and smelling of pine and lime soap. A tall glass of water sat beside an almost empty bag of Sage's ginger strips. He'd made himself at home, but not overly so and she liked his restraint, his awareness of borders.

"I made the mistake of opening them before I left Marietta, and then eating them all the way here," he said, pushing the chocolates toward her in silent invitation.

"We've all made that mistake." She took *one*, and vowed to resist the rest. "You want a tour of the house? People usually do. The architect was a Norwegian who settled here as a young man. He had a thing about honoring the landscape and the materials it provided. Revolutionary back then."

"A tour would be fine."

"And then we should probably decide what we're going to do this evening." Not that she was being directive. Or bossy. Or anything.

Much.

Ella swung into tour guide mode, leading Sawyer through the house to the front door. The tour started on the wide entry porch that had been built to look imposing and to complement the landscape and the stunning mountain views that the house commanded. She showed him the reception room with its rough-hewn wooden furniture and exposed wooden beams. She drew him through into the lounge for more exposed beams and a bank of floor-to-ceiling windows. She took him into her father's study where her mother's portrait hung, for no other reason than that she wanted her mother to get a good look at this man with his wide shoulders and dimpled smile, this man who Ella was in lust with.

Sawyer studied the portrait openly before looking back at her with a question in his eyes.

"Cameron Sawyer meet Caroline Grace Emerson. My mother."

He didn't comment that her mother was very beautiful, which she was, or that Ella favored her in looks, which she did. He didn't talk about the diamonds and sapphires at her mother's throat and in her ears.

"She looks happy," he murmured.

"I think she was. She and my father were so very much in love. At least, that's how I remember them. What about your parents, Sawyer? Are they still in love?"

"I don't know." Sawyer smiled faintly. "They seem well suited. Compatible."

"Is your mother happy?"

Again he hesitated. "My mother's very reserved. Hard to know what she's thinking or feeling."

"How long since you've seen her?"

"Three years, maybe four."

"You should try and see her more often."

"Now you're being bossy."

"Guess I am. Still, she is your mother. Maybe you should think of her as an underutilized strategic resource."

"Yeah, no. Pretty sure that's not going to work either. How about I say that I hope she's happy and leave it at that?"

"We're really quite different when it comes to family, aren't we?"

"You noticed."

Hard not to, thought Sawyer grimly, and hot on *that* thought came the notion that now would be a good time to tell Ella what he needed to tell her about his family. He looked to the window, at the snow now falling thick and fast. Ella followed his gaze and frowned.

"What are your thoughts on eating in and staying overnight?" she asked. "Because I have a sneaking suspicion that unless we leave now we're probably not going to get out.

And even if we do get out, I'll probably not get back in tonight. Or you could go and I could stay," she added belatedly.

"Where's your father?"

"He went to Livingstone with a load of hay. He'll either be back soon or he'll stay put for the night."

Sawyer frowned. He'd been perfectly willing to annoy Ella's father, what with his continued interest in Ella and the kissing in the park, but this was a whole new level of inappropriate behavior.

"We won't be completely alone," she offered next. "Carl and Jem live in the bunkhouse by the barn and there's a rope line between them and the barn and the house. It's under snow, but it'll pull up if anyone needs to get about in a whiteout."

Better, but only slightly.

"I'm really sorry to put you in such an awkward position."

"You keep worrying about my reputation. Do you ever worry about yours?"

"Er… mine's pretty sound," she offered lamely.

"You barely know me." That was the crux of it. "You don't know who you're getting mixed up with, Ella."

"Reese employed you."

"*He* barely knows me."

"Mardie trusts you."

"Are you really going to trust Mardie's instincts when it

comes to men?"

"Ray gave you a room."

"In a truck stop bunkhouse." He glanced outside again. "Will that calf be okay out there in that?"

"Ha!" she said. "You can't imply that you're bad news with one breath and ask about the welfare of the calf in the next. That's not how it works."

"Could be a ruse."

"Could be, but I trust my instincts. The cow and calf will be fine. They're in a well sheltered pocket – that's why it was so important to get them there this afternoon. As for us staying here tonight—" Ella shrugged. "Whether my father returns or not, I figure we'll be fine too."

"Where do you get your certainty from, Ella?"

"No one ever showed me how to be any different." She glanced up at her mother's portrait and then quickly looked away. "It's a turn-off, isn't it?"

"No."

This time her glance was for him and it was a startled one. For all her bravado and strength, Ella Grace Emerson had some vulnerabilities too.

"No, it's not a turn-off. Don't ever change."

"Oh. So."

"Couple of things I need to tell you about, Ella. About me. About my family. Before we settle in for the night."

"Good things?"

"No."

"Yeah, didn't think so. Do we need wine? I think we need wine. And a fire in the living room and a casserole in the oven." And then the phone on her father's desk phone began to ring. Ella reached out and picked up.

Her father, unless Sawyer had missed his guess.

He listened as Ella told her father that she'd shifted the pregnant cows to the shelter of the foothills and that there was a calf on the ground already. She told him that, yes, Carl and Jem had shifted the rest of the stock to more sheltered locations. She told him she'd see him in the morning.

"You didn't tell him I was here," Sawyer said when she hung up.

"Wouldn't want to worry him unnecessarily."

"Ella." There was a warning in there somewhere.

"You need to let people make their own mistakes," she told him firmly. "Living room fire, do you think?"

Maybe he did need to let people make their own mistakes.

Ella shot him a quick smile and headed for the kitchen. Sawyer headed for the living room and lit the fire. Five minutes later he found her standing in front of the wine rack in the kitchen, looking thoroughly undecided.

"This is getting ridiculous," she said. "There's more wine in the cellar, but if I go down there I could take hours. First I'm wardrobe challenged and now the wine."

"Maybe you're simply tired and in need of a little rest and relaxation." Maybe he should leave his confessions for another time.

Yeah, no.

He reached around her, pulled a Shiraz cabernet from the rack and tucked it in her hand. "This one. Not too old, not too new, good body and smooth as silk going down."

"Thank you, bartender. I appreciate it."

He opened the bottle and poured into the two large wine glasses sitting on the bench beside a still frozen loaf of crusty bread.

"Beef casserole's in the oven."

"Great. It'll go with the wine."

They returned to the living room. Ella lit the candelabra – one set on either side of that enormous window, another set on a side table beside the doorway through to the hall.

"In case of a power outage?" he asked as he sat on the bank of lounge chairs that ran the length of the room. Enough room for eight people to sit comfortably. As for seating two…

"Not really in case of power outage." Ella settled in beside him, wine glass I hand. "We've a generator and plenty of flashlights. A lot of the time we light the candles because people like the atmosphere."

"Of yesteryear?"

"Yeah."

"Feels like church."

Another quick grin split her firelit face. "Cozy confessional. You wanted to tell me something but we were interrupted and waylaid."

Sawyer hesitated.

"Or we could just talk about regular things. Like how long you plan to stay in Marietta?"

An easy question.

Until he factored in her.

"I have another three week's work at the saloon before Reese's regular bartender returns."

"You're better at bartending than Josh is."

"I don't want his job."

She gave him a measured look. "Where will you go after that?"

"Washington State." And at her enquiring look, "I have a house there."

"You have a house?"

"Bought and paid for. I've lived there exactly three weeks out of the past fifty-two. It's not really working out."

"Why not?"

"I thought I wanted it. But." There was always a *but.* "It's a little out of the way. It sits on a cliff overlooking the Pacific, just outside a sleepy little seaside town."

"I guess *parts* of that equation might fit with what I know of you," she offered dubiously. "I'm liking the view I've got going in my imagination."

"It does have good views. Nothing quite as spectacular as your views, but the ocean has its own charm."

"Do you surf and swim?"

"Yes."

"It's starting to make a little more sense."

"There's a really good wood-fired-oven pizza place in the town," he offered. "Little hole in the wall operation. In the mornings they do six different types of bagels."

"Now you're talking."

They lapsed into silence.

Now, he thought. Tell her now.

But he sipped at his wine and stared into the fire instead.

"What kind of work will you do there?" she finally said.

"The lower floor is set up as a business hub, with a formal meeting room, high-speed communications, records room, and plenty of workspace. The idea was – is – to use it as a base and get more strategic when it comes to the company restructuring jobs I take. Get in, get out, finish up the work from home. Although that has its drawbacks too."

"Sawyer, you mystify me. You're comfortably situated with a home and well-paid work that you seem to be able to take or leave at whim. Forgive me for being wildly impolite, but are you rich?"

"It's all relative, don't you think?"

"Yeah, no."

"I come from an extremely wealthy background but I started again from scratch. I'm not even in the same league as the rest of my family, but I'm certainly not destitute by any means."

"So you *are* rich."

"Yes."

"So why on earth are you working at Grey's and living in a bunkhouse?"

"Nobody gets that, do they?"

Ella shook her head.

"I like working at the saloon. Coming into a new place and figuring out what makes everyone tick and how they fit together. I like finding out what's important to people and what's not. It helps me do my other job – the one where I look at revenues and deals and then start ripping up management plans. Spread a business out on paper and it's all too easy to forget that we're playing with people's lives."

Now it was Ella's turn to look at the fire.

"What do you do when people fall for you, Sawyer? Either as a bartender or in your corporate magician incarnation? You're rich. You're smart. You're absolutely gorgeous and of marriageable age. Why aren't you hooked up?"

There. Right there was the opening he needed. And he knew damn well that Ella had given it to him deliberately. "Confession time, huh?"

"Your call."

It was time. Past time. "There was a girl. My girl."

Ella sipped at her wine and listened.

"Zoey was twenty-one, I was twenty-four and we were living together. I'd asked her to marry me."

"And she said no and broke your heart?"

"She said yes and made me very happy."

"Hnh," said Ella. "So much for that theory."

"Problem was, my brother wanted her too, and at the engagement party he stood up and told everyone that she was carrying his child and that she needed to marry him and not me. It was a complete lie. I knew it. Zoey knew it. My mother suspected it. But."

"But?"

"You don't know my brother. He had a lot of power, even back then. A lot of people positioned inside his web. He was very convincing."

"I hate him already."

Sawyer smiled wryly. "Zoey and I went ahead with our engagement, regardless. Richard didn't get what he wanted that night, but the damage it did to Zoey's reputation was irreversible. The gossip mongers attacked her."

"Tell me she stuck it out."

"Would you have?"

"Yes."

"For a month, she did. Zoey's no weakling. But it was a month during which my brother pursued her relentlessly; never mind that she wanted nothing to do with him; never mind that Zoey lived with me. He'd corner her on her way to work and on the way home, and when I started taking her to work and picking her up he'd get to her *at* work. He was at every social function we went to and he was obnoxious.

And then…" Sawyer cleared his throat. "Then he tried to rape her. To make the statement he'd made at our engagement party true."

"Oh."

There was a world of sick horror in Ella's quiet exclamation. And Sawyer let it sit there.

"Anyway, that was the end of it for Zoey. She'd had enough. She was living in fear. I wanted her to press charges, but she broke the engagement and took off back to her family in Spain instead. In the end she did it with my blessing. Zoey's fine now. She's safe. She's married and very much in love with her husband, who adores her."

"Didn't your brother follow her?"

"No. As soon as Zoey broke our engagement Richard lost interest in her. But he hadn't quite finished with me. We were working in the family business, him in management, me in marketing – mainly because we were better off working apart. I'd had some success marketing one particular product we'd developed. A mixer – alcohol lite. It did good things for our bottom line. My father liked that and praised me for it. Richard and I had grown up with him getting all the praise and me getting none, so it was a big thing. A big change."

"Why did your father never praise you?"

"I think maybe he wanted to at times, but there was always Richard and the fear of what might set him off. Even as a kid he was uncontrollable." Especially as a kid.

He took a breath, let it out. "My brother framed me for embezzlement and presented the evidence to my father. My father didn't want to believe him, but he couldn't get his head around the notion that Richard had framed me either. He couldn't believe that anyone could carry that much hate. Easier to believe that I got stupid and greedy."

"Your father is a very foolish man."

"You *are* black and white, aren't you?"

"He should have dug to the bottom of it. The lies, the attempted rape… all of it. And *you*… maybe you should have stayed and fought for your rights and for your place within family."

But Sawyer just shook his head. "It was tearing my family apart."

"So you just up and left?"

You don't sound impressed.

"Jesus, Sawyer." She reached for a fat cushion and smacked him with it. It wasn't particularly soft. "You let him *win*."

"I have a good life."

"Without *family*. Though by the sound of it they weren't worth much anyway. How could they stand by and watch that happen, Sawyer? How?"

"There's big business involved. Someone had to take the fall for the embezzlement."

"How about *nailing the person who did it*?"

"My father made his choice."

"Your father's a moron."

Yep. Definitely black and white. Not that he didn't enjoy Ella's indignation and her fire on his behalf, because, well…

Maybe he had an ever-so-mild craving for fierce, blind trust.

"Is that it?" she wanted to know. "Any more skeletons?"

"No, I think we're done."

"Oh, we are anything but done." Ella set down her wine-glass on the little side table. She took Sawyer's and set it there too, and then she was sliding into his lap, all warm and fragrant woman. "We've barely begun, and you don't scare me, Cameron Sawyer. You and your screwed up family."

"You're something else, you know that, don't you?"

"Do you like it? Do you like what I am?"

"Yes."

"Then let's get back to where we were at the park, shall we? You were showing me a few things about lust."

She'd just shown him a few things about loyalty and acceptance and there was every chance that she'd break him, regardless of relative size, but he summoned a smile and tried to get with the plan. But not before one last word of warning.

"He's still out there, Ella. My brother and his world of hate."

"I hear you. And now I want to touch you." She followed her words with the brush of her fingers across his shoulders. "Fill up on you." A kiss for the edge of his lips and then another, more centered and a moist lick of tongue.

"Learn what makes you tremble and what makes you blush. We good?"

"Yeah." It was just lust, this trembling in his hands as he reached for her. Base need, not reverence, as he buried his hands in her silky dark hair and returned her kiss. "We're good."

"What would you take from me, Sawyer, if your brother wasn't hovering in the shadows? Would you want love as well as the lust? Would you be freer with your own heart?"

"Probably." She stole a kiss and then another. "Yes."

"Would you claim a home for yourself? Would you settle?"

"I might." She scraped her teeth along his jaw and reached for the buttons on his shirt. "Yes."

"You do know that I'm taking everything you say with a grain of salt, given that I'm seducing you while you're saying it?"

"Good idea," he managed hoarsely, for the pad of her thumb had just stroked over one of his nipples.

"Last question, I promise," she whispered, and he groaned, because her hands had found his belt buckle and both body and brain heartily approved. "Have you ever thought of starting your own family? Have you ever dreamed of babies to love and a woman who'd fight for you and love you and stand by your side, no matter what?"

"No." While the candles flickered with revelation and his heart broke wide open. "Yes."

Chapter Seven

ELLA KNEW WHERE she wanted him. Stretched out naked on the rug in front of the fire, with cushions and blankets all around him and his body a study of shadow and light. It had been a good look for him in her imagination. Enough to make her all flustered and needy.

The reality was even better.

"Let me," she murmured, as she put her hand to his chest and encouraged him to ease back against the pile of cushions. "Can I?" she pleaded, as she drew his arms above his head and circled his wrists with his fingers and then dragged her nails back down his arms, skirting the outside of his armpits and then on to the muscles along the outer edges of his torso. Lines that ran in to his waist and then down over the cut of his hips and the silky skin of his inner thighs, and, oh, the noises he made. The ragged, jagged breath. "You're so beautiful," she whispered.

"That's my line."

Ella leaned over him, hands to either side of him now, and ghosted her breath across one of his nipples and watched it pebble tight. "I want another line." She used the tip of her tongue to wet it, tease it, and finally to suck it into her mouth before releasing it with a pop. "A better line."

"Take your clothes off."

Sawyer had undressed women before, if his expertise in that area was anything to go by. And then he rolled her on her stomach, brushed her hair to one side of her neck and put his lips there and lit her up completely.

"Lust," he said in a voice that promised heaven. "Needs to be built."

And then he trailed his lips down her back, finding all the best places. Spots that made her gasp and squirm and heat up and grow moist. He lifted her up as her knees shifted into place beneath her and his big hands kneaded her buttocks, exposing her, playing her to perfection as he slid one hand lower until his thumb found the exact right spot and circled it.

She pressed into the touch, eager for more. She'd become a wanton whimpering woman and she loved it. "Sawyer?" He added a blunt knuckle to the mix, giving her something to grind down on and, oh, sweet mercy, she needed it, needed more.

So this was lust. Blind, mind-altering desire because why else would she be moistening her lips and spiraling beneath his touch, no intercourse required.

"Not yet, not yet, not yet," she whimpered.

"You can go again," he murmured, and then he was

shifting around, his lips trailing over her buttocks before joining his fingers, gliding a path straight to her clitoris and taking over from his thumb. She screamed out, no inhibitions left, as hands and tongue brought her to soaring, trembling completion.

He let her topple sideways after that, onto blankets and pillows as he settled down on his back beside her, farthest from the fire, smug as a well fed wolf.

Ella felt her own lips tug into a smile at his obvious state of readiness. She'd get to that soon, just as soon as her sated body started moving again and her lungs had enough air. "Be right with you."

"Relax." He eased back onto one elbow and curled around her, his knees tucked in under her buttocks. "I'm not going anywhere."

Not tonight, at any rate. She took his hand and threaded his fingers through her own. She let her eyes grow slumberous as she memorized every curve and plane of his body. And then slowly, deliberately, she slid her hand over the outside of his, raised it to her lips and licked a long stripe across the center of his palm. "Show me," she said, and wrapped his hand and hers around his erection.

The effect on Sawyer was instantaneous. His eyes closed, he bit his lip and a ripple ran straight through him. She'd never seen a more responsive man. "Kink?"

"Big one." As he set up a slow stroking rhythm, his grip firm and his body pushing into it. Ella looked, debated, and then set about adding the swipe of her thumb to the head on the upstroke. And then, well, maybe she had to leave him to it while she brought her hand back to her lips and tasted.

The sounds he made were another feast for her senses. "I think we might need condoms now," she murmured. "Please tell me you have some."

He rolled back and reached for his jeans, and she let him coat up before sliding into place on top of him, wriggling until she felt the press of him against her and then dipping inside. She shifted slightly at the insistent pressure, for he was proportional everywhere and no one could ever accuse him of being a slight man.

"Easy," he murmured, stilling beneath her and running a gentle hand down her side, but Ella didn't want easy, she wanted *him*. Now. And inch by all-encompassing inch she made it so.

Ella had never felt so full, every sense engaged, drilling into her, he was all around her. She'd never had her senses be so completely engaged. And then she put her hands to his hips and lifted all the way up and then slid back down, reveling in the friction and the drag, a drag Sawyer facilitated by splaying one hand low over her stomach and pressing down on her clitoris with his thumb.

"You're right." She closed her eyes and bit down on her lip to stop the helpless noises from escaping. "I *can* go again."

And then Sawyer began to move and Ella surrendered

herself to him completely.

Lust.

Lost.

Love.

By the time they were done, Ella had felt them all.

"MIDDLE NAME?" ELLA asked as they ate dinner in front of the fire some time later. She was dressed, sort of, in that she had her underwear on. Sawyer had opted for jeans, no shirt, and she wasn't complaining.

"Franklin."

"Seriously?"

"Ask my mother. I have no idea why."

"Favorite movie?"

"It's got hobbits in it."

"Best friend?"

Sawyer hesitated. "Zoey Alvarez."

Spanish surname. *My* woman, he'd called her. *The* woman. The one who'd been driven away. Ella didn't like the twinge of jealousy that went through her but it was there. "Are you still in love with her?"

"No."

"Sure?"

"Very sure." He held her gaze with a steady one of his own.

Okay, then. Maybe she really did need to let go of that

jealousy. Sawyer and Zoey had shared good times and bad times. The worst times. The bond between them might not be love anymore but it was always going to be strong. "Okay, I can work with that. Favorite type of music?"

"New Orleans Jazz. Sometimes Bluegrass. Yours?"

"Country," she told him. "And then Western."

He grinned at her. "We're going to have to fix that."

"Greenhorn, you can try."

Ella didn't quite know how this led to them ending up in bed again, her bed this time.

But it did.

Chapter Eight

MORNING-AFTERS WERE PROBLEMATIC, decided Sawyer, as Samuel T. Emerson stepped through into the kitchen from the side door and stopped dead.

It was half ten and the roads were supposedly still under a foot and a half of snow, although perhaps not anymore, given that Ella's father was definitely, undeniably here. Sawyer was here too, smelling of sex and this man's daughter, and he was pretty sure he had a bite mark on his stomach, just above the cut of his hip.

And another one on his shoulder.

Ella was in the shower.

Ella had woken him at dawn to listen to the weather report, because apparently cowgirls did that, and then she'd burrowed back down into the bed clothes hooked an arm over his chest and slid straight back to sleep. Sawyer had gathered her closer, buried his face in her hair and done the same.

They'd woken again not ten minutes ago. Sawyer had come down for coffee and a shower of his own, and, yep,

Samuel T. Emerson was still standing there.

Eyes narrowed.

"I see you got the position," Samuel said.

"Kind of not thinking about it in quite those terms, Samuel," he offered quietly.

"What kind of terms *are* you considering?"

Good question. Sawyer ran a hand though his hair, not entirely sure it would do in lieu of a comb. Samuel's gaze fixed on a spot of skin just under his arm, a place Ella had really liked, Sawyer looked down and hastily lowered his arm because… more marks.

Awkward.

"You want to go and put a shirt on, son?"

And then Ella barreled in, dressed, thank God, took in the scene and smile brightly.

"I *thought* I heard someone pull up," Ella said casually. "Did you get a look at the group two steers on the way?"

"They're fine," her father replied dryly. "Aren't you going to introduce me to your friend?"

"Haven't you already met?"

"Ella," her father said, and the one word warning was enough to set her back some. Not so confident now as she backed up and began the introduction.

"Cameron Sawyer, this is my father, Samuel T. Emerson. Daddy, this is Cameron. Cameron kept me company last night."

Her father's eyebrows rose. Ella held his gaze with a

steady one of her own. "Is now a good time to tell you that if I have my way he'll be doing it again?"

Sawyer would have probably chosen a different time, but that was just him.

"How about you get an old man a coffee, Ella, while I think on it?" her father said gruffly, before turning a carefully neutral gaze on Sawyer. "What do you think of the place?"

"It's beautiful."

"Impressive?"

"That too."

"Best valley on God's green earth. Where are you from, Cameron?"

"Sydney. Noosa. Copper Creek. Brisbane."

"And Washington state," said Ella, moving in and reaching around him for the jar of coffee grounds.

"Not exactly a stable existence."

"No."

"Glad to see we're all getting along," said Ella. "But I think I might have left something in the living room, so…" She glanced up at Sawyer. "I just have to go and do a couple of things. In the living room."

Most of their clothes were still scattered across the living room. The wine was heaven knew where. Good idea for someone to get to them before her father did. And Ella was the only one who knew where all the rugs and cushions went.

Well, except for her father. Sawyer gave her an almost

imperceptible nod.

"Grab his shirt while you're there," said her father.

Guess no one had ever accused Samuel T. of being slow.

"Go," Sawyer nudged her with his shoulder as Ella's cheeks went bright red. "Your father and I can stay here and bond."

"Is that likely?" she murmured.

"Notice that I'm willing to try."

Ella shot her father a quick glance, and then stood on tiptoe and kissed Sawyer's cheek. "Thank you." Her smile could have gotten him to do just about anything.

He was so screwed.

Ella left. Her father stayed and took a seat at the kitchen bench. Still awkward. "How do you take your coffee, Samuel?"

"Strong and black, with one."

Sawyer made the coffee in silence and sat it down in front of the other man. He was used to serving others. He saw no slight in it. If he were in Samuel T's shoes he'd want a coffee too.

The older man left the coffee on the bench and ran his hand across his mouth instead. "Wish my wife was here," he offered at last. "Twenty years she's been gone and I still miss her every damn day."

Sawyer hadn't tended bar on and off for years without learning a thing or two about encouraging another person to share. "Ella showed me her portrait."

"That wasn't her. It's too serene. Caroline could walk into a room and set my world on fire."

That'd be right, thought Sawyer. It was hereditary. "Mr. Emerson, I'm not about to tell you that this isn't what it looks like. It's exactly what it looks like. As for where it's going I can't say, because I don't know. But I won't hurt your daughter. I'll put myself on the line before I do that."

Samuel T. reached for his coffee. "Maybe that's all a father can ask."

SAWYER NEVER MEANT for him and Ella to become inseparable, but one week passed and then another, and not a day had gone by without talking to her on the phone or seeing her at the saloon or in the mornings before he started work. By mid-morning Ella had usually already put in half a day's work at the ranch and had no hesitation when it came to sauntering into the truck yard and hammering on his door. Her father didn't think it was a good look for her.

Sawyer agreed.

Not that Ella had taken the slightest notice of either of them. Short of buying or renting a house in Marietta, there was nothing to do but start getting up and into town earlier and texting Ella his whereabouts before mid-morning, or if she was short a hand, heading on out to the ranch. She was still trying to make a cowboy out of him. He was still telling her it was never going to happen, but the truth was he enjoyed the physicality of it and he *loved* seeing Ella in her element.

He had a midday start at the saloon today but he was meeting Ella for an early lunch at the deli. He'd been expecting to see her in her usual work wear, but today she'd gone all dynasty princess on him and was wearing good jeans and boots, a pretty shirt, and jewelry.

"What's the occasion?"

"Ball gown shopping at the local bridal wear shop," she offered glumly. "And trust me that never ends well. By the way, I have a spare ticket for the Valentine's Ball at the Graff Hotel next weekend. It's a big affair. Huge. Think ballrooms and chandeliers, fairy lights, pink champagne and feathers."

"Feathers?"

"Okay, I'm not sure about the feathers, but it's to launch a big competition. They're giving away a wedding. Do you have a formal suit?"

"Er…"

"For the ball, not the wedding," she offered somewhat dryly. "Although I'm pretty sure that Mr. Armani or some-one of his ilk is going to tailor-make you a wedding suit, should you win the competition."

"How do I win the competition?" he asked warily. "I don't just have to walk through a doorway or something, do I?"

"You and your significant other would have to write a persuasive five-hundred word essay on why you want to get married. And then agree to a whole flood of publicity."

"I'd rather elope."

"I'm sure you're not alone. Meanwhile, I need a gown. Maybe even a pink gown. Possibly with feathers. Or sparkles. Or something."

"Good luck."

"And *you*, should you choose to accompany me, will need a suit."

"With feathers?"

"I think not. Will you come? Will you even be here?"

There was an underlying thread of anxiety to her words that Sawyer didn't like. "I finish up at the saloon Tuesday week. Nothing stopping me from heading to my place on the Wednesday, picking up a suit, airing the place out, and being back here on Friday. You can come too, if you want?"

"I do want." Ella's wistful expression confirmed it. "But we've a new bull buyer coming to the ranch on Thursday and my father's away. May I take a rain check?"

"You may."

She leaned forward, over the table, and kissed him square on the lips in front of half of Marietta, Montana, and Sawyer grinned and slid his hand in her hair and made it count.

"It's not working, this attempt of yours to cultivate a bad girl image," he said when she pulled back. "Too many people around here have known you since birth. I live in a truck stop bunkhouse and work behind a bar. I'm a lean, mean flirting machine and I'm becoming respectable by association."

"You don't flirt anymore, according to Mardie."

"She lies."

"Will you come to the ball?"

"Yes."

"Can I come to your bunkroom tonight?"

"*Hell*, no."

"You're as bad as my father." She sat back, her gaze speculative and her smile playful. "Did I mention that my father's away?"

TUESDAY AFTERNOON AND the end of Sawyer's stint behind the bar at Grey's Saloon rolled around all too soon. Reese offered him on-call work and guaranteed him Friday and Saturday nights if he wanted them. Mardie thumped him on the arm hard and got alarmingly teary-eyed when he told Reese, no.

"She'll be fine," Reese said as she stalked from the kitchen. "She just doesn't want you to go. Figure you might have a few people in that position." Reese's gaze sharpened. "Come on through to the office. I want to show you something Jason found on the Web this morning. Breaking news."

The news was… significant.

Richard Sawyer – businessman and CEO of JB Brewing Industries—was going down. Embezzlement, forgery, three counts of assault occasioning actual bodily harm, one count of sexual assault, and an apprehended personal violence order taken out against him that cited intimidation, harassment, stalking, and more assault. And they'd still granted him bail. Laurence Sawyer, former CEO and major shareholder of JB Brewing, had been given conditional board approval to step in and mop up. The predominantly family-owned brewery was on the brink of collapse, blah blah, blah blah. The scavengers and speculators were having a field day.

Sawyer sat back in the office chair and blew out his breath. He felt sick just looking at it. "Does Jason know that he's my brother?"

Reese nodded. "He dug a little deeper after reading that."

"Tell him you can't pick your relatives."

"He knows." Reese smiled thinly. "Does Ella know your family background?"

"She knows some of it." Sawyer shoved a hand through his hair. "My brother's been heading in this direction since—" God, even as a kid, the things Richard had done to get his own way had been extreme. "Long as I can remember."

"Where do you stand in all of this?" Reese nodded toward the monitor.

"Out of it." And yet... "Doesn't matter how far you run, does it? When it comes to family you're never really gone."

IT TOOK SAWYER ten minutes to throw his gear in the pickup, and eleven and a half hours to get to his Washington home. From there he phoned his mother, and there was no *hello* or *how are you?* forthcoming, just a quietly defeated, "You've heard."

"Yeah."

"I did a very foolish thing when you left. I never told you. I was so *angry* with your father for brushing Richard's actions aside. As for Richard, then and now..." Her voice broke. "How did I create such a person, Cameron? What did I *do?*"

Sawyer closed his eyes on the view from his bedroom window. A sweeping ocean view. "He just was."

"When you left, I sold half our shares in the brewery and put the proceeds in trust for you. They were mine to sell, so I did it. Your father and Richard have been struggling to control the business ever since. I think that's what pushed Richard over the edge."

"What he did to Zoey was already over the edge."

"They granted him bail."

He couldn't keep his bitterness down any longer. "Did it ever occur to you that maybe you should have left him behind bars?"

"Yes." He could barely hear her. "I wasn't the one who paid Richard's bail. Nor did your father. He got the money from somewhere. Nowhere good."

"Buy back into the business, Mother. You'll probably

make money if you buy in now. Give Dad the control he needs to run things his way."

"No. That money is for you."

"It's what I'd do."

"Then come home and do it."

"Mum—"

"Cameron, I'm at the end of my rope. Your father's barely sleeping, Richard's God knows where and I don't know how much longer I can hold this together. You've always been the strongest of us all. The best of us. Come back to us, please, if you could just consider it."

"I have a life here. A woman I don't want to leave behind." There, he'd admitted it. "You're asking me to walk her into that?"

"No. I—no." His mother sounded defeated. "I didn't realize."

Sawyer paced. He'd been pacing ever since he picked up the phone.

"I'll let you go," she murmured.

"I'll come alone. I'll give you one month and I can be there by mid next week, but I can't help you if you don't cooperate. Buy back the stock. Get me a seat on the board. I'll send you my CV. Tell my father to give that to the board as well. Tell him I'll not be his yes man but I will support good management decisions. Tell him I know damn well that he's always been good at those. Unless it involved Richard."

"Richard—"

"Deserves what he gets."

"Cameron, we do this and he'll come after you. I'm not guessing. I'm sure."

"I know. Where does he think I am now?"

"I don't think he knows."

"Tell him I'm on my way. And I will be, just give me a few days. Tell him I want my life back. And I want my family back, and I want to be able to offer the woman I love safety and security rather than a life full of fear. I'm not coming home to hold Richard's hand, Mother. I am done with staying out of his way. I'm coming home to finish him."

Chapter Nine

S AWYER HAD LEFT. Ella heard the news third-hand when she went to Emerson's Transport on Wednesday morning to find him. She wasn't impressed. Gutted, more like. Upset enough to call in on Mardie at the saloon. Mardie, who'd taken one look at her and told Reese she was taking her lunch break now and had then proceeded to sit Ella down in front of a plate of fried food.

Sawyer phoned her while she was still at the bar contemplating the delights of fried onion rings dipped in mayonnaise. He was at his beach house in Washington. Ella didn't even know the name of the town, and it seemed a little late to ask.

"I didn't think you were leaving quite so soon. Couldn't you have said goodbye?"

Mardie nodded vigorous agreement. Damn right he could have said goodbye.

"I'll be back on Friday – with a suit for the ball. I wasn't exactly thinking in terms of goodbye."

"You weren't?" Now she sounded tentative as well as

needy.

"I just have to sort out a couple of things while I'm here. I will be back, Ella. Don't give my ticket away."

"I won't."

"See you soon."

"Yeah."

And then he was gone.

Ella met Mardie's troubled gaze with one of her own. "He said he'd be back in time to take me to the ball."

"Yeah?" Mardie's face brightened.

"Do you think he will be?"

Mardie nodded. "Sawyer says he's going to do something, he does it. That's my experience of him. What's yours?"

"Same."

"See? We can't *both* be wrong."

Ella smiled wryly. "Pretty sure we can."

Mardie rolled her eyes. "Hey, Reese. Is Sawyer going to get back here in time for Friday's ball?"

"Ask him," said Reese.

"See?" Mardie picked up a fried onion ring, dragged it through the mayonnaise and offered it to Ella, dripping and all. "Reese says he'll be here, and Reese is male and *never* wrong."

"I heard that," muttered Reese. "Don't you have work to do?"

"See?" Mardie murmured sagely. "Never. Wrong."

Ella worked herself to exhaustion for two days solid, until on Friday lunchtime, her father ordered her to get on up to the house and stay there and get ready for the ball.

"I haven't heard from him these past two days," she muttered, and her father stopped stacking hay and regarded her narrowly. "At all."

"Phone him."

"You think I should? He said he'd be here. I don't want him to think that I don't trust him to keep his word."

Ella's father just looked at her.

"You know he's not in Marietta anymore?"

"Ray said." Her father took his cap off and wiped at his brow with the sleeve of his shirt. "Still. I presume he owns a phone?"

Ella nodded.

"Text him. Ask him what time he'll be here."

"Oh, that's clever."

"Yeah," her father drawled dryly. "I'm Einstein."

"Could be I'm feeling just a *little* insecure." Ella held up her forefinger and thumb about an inch apart and watched her father smile. "But I will. I'll text him. I'm not sure I ever gave him a time we had to be there."

The doors opened at 7 pm. Before that, there were drinks in the bar. Dancing commenced at eight. At some point during the evening someone would launch Marrietta's Great Wedding Giveaway competition. As far as Ella was concerned, as long as they turned up before pumpkin hour she could still say she'd been to the ball.

Although turning up a few hours *before* midnight would be better. "I'll call."

"That's my girl."

But when she called, Sawyer's phone was either turned off or out of range.

Ella picked her way through a late lunch and then decided she needed to make bean soup with ham hocks. She took a shower once it was simmering gently, but there was no sense putting on her ball gown yet. She had soup to stir and biscuits to make first.

Her father came in just at six, took one look at her and the soup and the kitchen counter covered in biscuits, and wisely headed for the emergency kitchen whisky instead. "Did you get hold of him?"

"Not yet. But he'll be here. He will. And then I'll get dressed." Ella pulled a fresh batch of biscuits from the oven and dumped them on the cooling rack on the counter. "Biscuit?"

Her father took a biscuit and wisely opted not to say another word.

Sawyer turned up just at dusk, wearing a suit tailor made for those magnificent shoulders and bearing an armful of mixed colored roses. He stood on the front porch, with the mountains in the background and Ella thought she'd never seen anything more magnificent.

"These are for you," he said and held them out to her.

"There would have been chocolates too, only Sage sold them because I didn't get there before closing time. And I don't know if you still want to go to that Valentine's ball with me or not, but we could." He took in her jeans and plaid shirt. "If you wanted to."

She took the flowers from him. "I've been waiting for your call."

"I did call."

"On *Wednesday*."

"Yeah, but I said I'd be back for the ball."

"It never occurred to you to phone again today and confirm it?"

"It did occur to me. There should be a message on your mobile. Or four."

"Oh." Still. "Mardie thinks I should skewer you for leaving without notice."

"Mardie's mean."

"My father hid all the shotguns."

"Smart man."

"It's a good thing I don't have an impulsive streak."

"Yeah. Hey, Ella." All of a sudden he looked uncertain. "Got a couple of things to mention. Updates, of a sort. The kind could impact on whether you want to go to the ball at all. With me."

Ella reached out and dragged him in and shut the door. "What do you mean?"

"Is your father in? Because maybe he needs to hear this

too."

"My father's in his study." And that was where she headed.

Her father took one look at them both and headed for
the whisky.

"Where's mine?" Ella said as she set the flowers on the
sideboard.

Silently her father poured two more.

"Here's the deal." The playful note in Sawyer's voice had
disappeared and about three ton of steel had taken its place.
"My older brother is going down for rape, corporate embezzlement, assault, and half a dozen other assorted felonies.
This isn't a surprise because he's done it all before." He
pinned Ella with a troubled green gaze. "Still want me to
take you to the ball?"

"Of course."

"I'm heading home next week to help save the family
brewing business. It's called JB Brewing and it holds a
significant global market share. It's not a small corporation
and I don't rightly know how long it will take to fix. I'd ask
you to come with me, but until Richard is behind bars its
best if you don't. It's not safe for you there."

It was a lot to take in. Ella ran a nervous hand around
the back of her neck and slid her father a glance. Her father
stared back, stony eyed. "Sawyer's brother isn't all that nice,"
she offered.

"So I gather."

"So, uh." There was a distinct possibility that she probably should have mentioned Sawyer's brother to her father earlier.

She turned her gaze back on Sawyer. "Who was she this time?"

"One of our corporate execs. The good news is that she pressed charges and has the will to see a nasty court case through. And then she'll probably sue JB Brewing."

"I'm inclined to say good for her."

Sawyer's lips hitched a little higher around the edges. "Let's just say she won't lack for support. The bad news is that Richard made bail. He's had to surrender his passport but I don't like it. He has a tendency to think that rules and regulations don't apply to him. If Richard finds out about you there's a chance he might come here looking for you, as a way to get to me. I've left him precious little else by way of leverage."

"I can handle it."

"Ella—

"I can."

"Here's a recent picture of him."

Ella took the paper Sawyer held out and studied his brother's handsome face before passing it to her father. Sawyer's brother didn't look like a power-tripping egomaniac, and that was probably part of the problem. "No one comes onto this place without our notice. We can show the photo to Jem and Carl, Ray, and the boys. If your brother comes poking around here we'll know it. And then we'll handle it. Right, Dad?"

Her father nodded, his eyes flat and hard.

Sawyer looked torn.

"Sawyer." She waited until his gaze had shifted from her father back to her. "You need to trust us on this – no going back to Australia and obsessing over what if. I'll be careful. We will *all* be on guard."

"Never meant to bring this kind of trouble down on you, Ella. Never wanted you to have to live in fear."

"This isn't fear."

"I'll fix it," he said raggedly. "I *will* neutralize him. Help put him behind bars, and then maybe *he* can get help, I don't know. And then I aim to come back and court you properly this time. Dinner and the movies. Weekends away somewhere special. Cows. Line dancing. Rodeos. The works."

Ella liked the sound of that. "You can line dance?"

"You can teach me."

"Where would you live?"

"I haven't really thought about it yet, but it's not a problem. I could keep the house on the coast, buy well in Marietta and still have change." This time Sawyer's words were for her father. "Sir, I'm not a pauper, whatever my former employment and living arrangements might have suggested. I can provide for your daughter."

Her father cleared his throat. "Ella could build here, on

the northern side of the ranch, tucked into the shelter of the foothills. We could build a new road out; that way there'd be more privacy for everyone involved."

"I'm right here," Ella said, before they decided to build her a castle. Although…

"We were just considering options," said her father.

Sawyer nodded. "Options."

First real smile she'd seen on his face all night. "Your dimples aren't always going to save you, Sawyer. If I go and get changed into my gown, I don't want to come back down here to find my future lodgings all organized for me, got it?"

Ella wanted *input* into those future house plans, dammit.

"Drink?" her father asked Sawyer pleasantly, pushing a glass toward him.

"I'm driving. Maybe something soft."

"Good thinking," she murmured. "Save your thirst for all that pink champagne."

"Maybe just the one whisky," she heard Sawyer say as she swept from the room before her smile split her face in two. Sawyer was back. Back with intent, and whether his brother aimed to make trouble or not, Ella wanted *this* Sawyer. The one who stood taller than before, and who looked at her with a world of quiet determination in his eyes. She wanted him just as much, if not more, than she'd wanted the old Sawyer.

And that was saying something.

Ella practically floated to her room and into her closet. She looked at the gown hanging against the wall and hit the ground with a thud. Lisa Renee from the bridal store had assured Ella that pale pink did wonderful things for her complexion and that the cut of this particular gown did amazing things for her figure. The sequins and the feathers, well, they were just for fun. They, too, were pale pink and there weren't that many of them. They were very discreet – sequins on the bodice, feathers at the hem. Elegant even.

What on earth had possessed her?

By the time Ella had put her makeup on, tried to do something with her hair and shimmied into her gown, she looked like a carnival kewpie doll. Oh, this was bad. Lisa Renee had good taste. Excellent taste. People *relied* on her to have good taste.

Clearly, when Lisa Renee had bought this she'd been having a meltdown.

Ella reached for her phone. Perhaps meltdowns were contagious.

"I'm looking at my gown and wondering whether *you're* going to want to go the ball with *me*," she offered when Sawyer picked up. "Too many feathers. And did I mention the sparkles?"

"I like sparkles. Did I mention that I've booked us a suite at Graff's Hotel?" he answered. "Two nights. The Valentine's package."

"And what might the Valentine's package include?"

"Turndown and chocolates, champagne breakfast in bed, a massage at some stage tomorrow, dinner at the hotel tomorrow night and a pink teddy bear."

Oh. Well. So. "I'll think about it," she muttered. "Don't go anywhere." And hung up.

Still, she hesitated. Fiddled some more with her hair and chose a perfume to dab at her wrists and behind her ears. Lisa Renee had persuaded her to buy pale pink stilettoes to go with the gown. Pale pink stilettoes for a woman who lived on a ranch. Ella let loose a nervous giggle. She was never shopping at Lisa Renee's again without at least two girl-friends in tow for backup.

At the last minute, she reached for a black velvet cape that tied at the neck with a black satin ribbon. It suited the gown. Gave it a fairytale air.

It was her mother's.

Ella stared at her reflection in the full length mirror and suddenly all she could see was her mother, a mother who she missed more than ever.

"You'd like him, Mama. I know you would. I think I love him."

Yeah, so there was that.

The sound of someone clearing his throat at her door made her whirl around, hand to her hair in nervous anticipation of it being Sawyer and that he'd just overheard her, but it was only her father.

"Oh, thank God."

"I left him nursing a whisky in the study," her father offered dryly. "I thought you might like to wear these." He held out a black velvet case and she knew before she even opened it that she would find her mother's diamond and ruby earrings nestled within. "You look beautiful, Ella Grace."

"Really?" She was starting to get a little teary.

"Really."

"He's a good man, Daddy. This other business with his brother and his family? He needs to go back and fix it. He'll be stronger for it."

"I'm not going to judge the man by the actions of his brother, Ella Grace. I'll judge him by his actions toward you."

"How's he doing so far?"

"It could've started better." He gestured toward the jewelry, and his eyes suddenly looked as watery as hers felt. "Take them. Don't be too long. Your man's down there climbing the walls waiting for you. I remember that feeling and not with a whole lot of fondness."

"I'll be there."

Her father left. Ella put her mother's jewelry on, repaired her eye makeup and took a deep breath as she stared at her reflection in the mirror. "You with me, Mama? You going to lend me your grace tonight?" Ella nodded. "Good, because I need it."

She smoothed her lipstick with her finger, wiped her fingers on a tissue and picked up her little black clutch. "Let's go get my man."

SAWYER DIDN'T SEEM to have much to say when he saw her. He looked and looked, but he just didn't seem to have any words. Then his face lit up with a smile that looked as if it came from within, and Ella felt a corresponding lightness sweep across her body. He liked it.

He liked her.

He cleared his throat, but there were still no words.

"He likes it," Samuel T. told her dryly.

"I really do." Sawyer had found his voice and it was rough and warm with a flattering thread of awe shot through it.

"Are you ready to go?" she asked.

"When you are."

Ella kissed her father on the cheek and then moved toward Sawyer. It felt right, moving toward this man with his broad shoulders and his troubled soul. "You look very respectable." She preferred him naked in front of the fire, but a black dinner suit and tie was an exceptionally fine alternative. "Tailor made?"

"The rack stuff doesn't fit. It's the shoulders."

"So I see." Ella ran an admiring gaze over him, delighted when he colored up just a little. "Are you worried about being recognized at the ball? In relation to your brother, I mean."

"Reese knows. And Jason Grey. Jasper Flint might have an inkling by now – he came by the bar the weekend before I

120

left and asked some fairly pointed questions."

"Do you *want* people to know who you are?" Ella thought in an important enough question to ask it before they got to the ball. "Who *else* you are?"

"I've never hidden my identity, Ella. I just haven't always advertised it, because people used to judge me in relation to Richard and I didn't like it. I daresay I won't like it any better this time around but it's still going to happen."

"Not around me."

Sawyer showed her his second genuine set of dimples for the night. "I can deal. I don't need protecting."

"So you think."

They left her father to his whisky and headed for Sawyer's ride. He'd swapped his battered pickup for a late model Audi fitted with snow tires. It was a beautiful vehicle, but it was going to take some skill getting it off the ranch without getting it stuck. Mind you, he'd somehow driven it in, so maybe there was hope for them yet.

Sawyer drove with a confidence born of great skill. He didn't have quite the relationship with speed that Ella had, but given the conditions maybe that was a good thing.

They had valet parking at the Graff Hotel this evening, that was new, and they also had a doorman and an attendant taking coats. "Promise you won't laugh," she murmured, tugging on the ribbon at her neck, the one that held her cape in place. And then the cape was gone and she stood there, revealed, and she hoped to heaven that the ballroom was as extravagantly decorated as she felt.

"Beautiful," said the coat attendant, and Sawyer nodded and offered his arm. Ella took it, uncertain of what the evening might bring but determined to not waste one more thought on feathers and the wearing of them. Ella liked feathers. End of story.

How they had managed to fill the Graff Hotel ballroom full to overflowing with people was anyone's guess, but they'd done it. The grand old room had kept its sculpted ceiling features and decadent chandeliers, but the down lights had been replaced by thousands of dangling fairy lights and pink and red themed decorations were everywhere. They had a band up on the stage and a podium for the making of announcements. Smack in the middle of the room stood a confectionery table, loaded with Valentine's Day candies.

"Does Marietta usually go all out for Valentine's Day?" Sawyer murmured, as a passing waiter offered them champagne, wine, sparkling water, or juice. Ella took the champagne, Sawyer took the juice.

"It's the launch. The one hundredth anniversary Great Wedding Giveaway. Here, read the poster." There was one pasted to the wall below a side chandelier. "The dress – very important."

"What type of dress would you choose?"

Maybe it was idle conversation but Ella gave it the consideration it deserved. "Something strapless and romantic. And, look, they even give you a selection of bridal nightwear."

"You really think a bride's going to need nightwear?"

"Your Neanderthal is showing."

"Guess I could work around the nightwear," he murmured. "Why the sudden interest in weddings?"

"Hey, I'm just reading the poster. The suit, flowers, hair and makeup, wedding cars, the wedding and reception venues, drinks and food, entertainment, the cake. What more does a happy couple need?"

"Lust?"

"You're so right. And love." Mustn't forget the essentials. "I still can't believe how many people are here and how glamorous everyone looks. I expect you've been to events like this before."

"A few."

"I'm trying very hard not to be too daunted by your other life and the people who populate it. And I'm not talking about your brother." Ella spotted another poster, this one situated behind the bar. A beer ad. And a JB beer brand. "Just how embroiled in the family business do you aim to get?"

Sawyer looked conflicted.

"You're going to be in it up to your armpits, aren't you?" She'd wanted a man who had other things going on in his life – business interests that didn't involve ranching. Could be she'd gotten a little more than she'd bargained for. "You're going to need that ground floor office space in your

Washington house. That's if you get back to the states at all."

"I said I'd be back." He leaned in close and his lips brushed her hair. "Have I ever given you cause not to trust me?"

"You mean apart from the masquerading as a rudderless drifter bartender?"

"I *was* a rudderless drifter bartender. And then I found something I wanted to keep and things changed." He looked down at her, his green eyes intent. "I'm not returning home because I want back in to the family business – I aim to help fix it and then get gone."

"But you could do more with it if you had a mind to. If you wanted to. Business is so global these days. You could probably work from anywhere. You could commute."

"From Marietta to Australia?"

"I hear people do it all the time."

He looked suitably amused. "You've heard no such thing."

"You could start a trend." Ella sighed and decided that subtlety was getting her nowhere. "All I'm saying is that if you get back to Australia and find that you need to spend a little longer there than you originally intended, you'd have my support. I know what home means and I know that sometimes people need to be there. I could visit you. I'm all about the travel."

Sawyer snorted. "You lie."

"For you I'd try."

"Ella." His voice had softened. "Australia isn't home for me – even if I call it that sometimes. Washington isn't home for me either – even though I have a house there. I'm going back to sort out family stuff because of what I want to be able to come back and offer you *here*."

"And, um." She wasn't waiting breathlessly for a wedding proposal. She *wasn't*. This sudden overwhelming desire to get married was simply the result of the wedding vibe all around them. "What might that be?"

He leaned closer, lips to her ear. "A life without fear. With me."

"Well, well. Isn't this cozy?"

The voice had enough oily venom in it to send a shudder straight through her. Sawyer went rigid and his gaze shot to hers in silent warning, but his movements were smooth as he straightened and turned toward the newcomer's voice.

"Richard," Sawyer said evenly.

"Hello, brother."

"I really didn't think you'd be stupid enough to come here." There were similarities in their big bodies and in their facial features, decided Ella, although Sawyer was bigger and more vibrant in every way. "You're wanted at home."

Richard's face contorted into an ugly sneer and he no longer resembled Sawyer at all. Not even a little bit. "You need to leave the folks at home to me."

"I don't think so."

"You know, I wondered, when I heard you were coming

back – after all these years – I wondered why? What would make my little brother return?"

"It appears I've been asked to clean up your mess."

"You think you're going to get a seat on the board and return the big hero – you're not," his brother warned. "You think that bitch is going to put me behind bars. She'll be lucky if she can testify. As for our beloved *parents*—" Richard almost spat the word. "They're mine. They've always been mine."

Sawyer had taken a step forward, getting all up into his brother's space, or maybe just trying to put Ella behind him, out of sight and away from his brother's notice.

Yeah, no.

Ella tilted her chin and stepped up beside Sawyer, elbow to elbow, presenting a united front. "Funny how times change," she said. "You must be Cameron's embezzling rapist brother."

"Oh, aren't you sweet." Richard's eyes glittered with a frenzy, that might have been chemical and might have been madness.

"You need to leave," Sawyer told him.

"What, and miss all this? Oh, I don't know. Maybe the little lady here can introduce me around. Love the feathers, by the way. So very showgirl. Do *you* pole dance?"

"I never did get the hang of it," she murmured sweetly, putting one hand firmly on Sawyer's suit-clad forearm to hold him back. "I was always too busy out on the range –

learning how to shoot. But if it's introductions you want, I'm sure I can help you. The sheriff's just over there, along with two of his deputies. And I know he's wearing a suit, but it looks a little bulky around the chest and chances are he's carrying concealed. Law men. They're just never off duty, are they?"

"Cameron, where did you find her? She's divine."

"And is that Reese over there next to Jason Grey? You'll love Reese. Ex-special forces. He's a bar manager now. Safest bar in Montana. You'd think he'd get sick of taking out scum, but it must just never get old."

Cameron had stepped back and taken her with him, slanting her a half-amused, half-warning glance. "Where'd you learn to trash talk, Ella?" he asked, pulling a phone from somewhere inside his jacket.

"You've never shown stud bulls, have you?"

"The mind boggles."

"Who are you calling?"

"My father's lawyer. He gave me this number to call. Something about Richard having had to surrender his passport as a condition of bail. Because if he leaves Australia, then it just gets messy, what with warrants and international borders and extradition orders and all that. And of course the breaking of bail conditions."

"All that just to deliver a threat?"

"I never said he was smart."

Ella looked up to find Richard melting away into the

crowd. "He's leaving."

Sawyer handed her the phone. "Wait here."

And then he was striding toward the exit, after his brother.

Ella headed for the sheriff and handed him the phone. "It's some lawyer in Australia," she told him. "Tell him Richard Sawyer's here in Marietta making threats against his brother, the woman he allegedly raped and his parents. I don't really know what happens next." She flashed the sheriff a bright smile, handed the man standing next to him her pink champagne and went after Sawyer.

Her father's pickup stood beneath the hotel portico, possibly awaiting the attention of valet parking, but she couldn't see her father anywhere.

Sawyer and his brother stood off to one side of the entrance, away from bright entrance lights and prying eyes. It probably wasn't wise to join them, given the cold and the wobbliness of high heeled shoes on icy ground, but she could stand witness, given Richard's liking for violence and aggression. Better to do this with eyes on them than not. And then Sawyer's brother saw her and smiled, and a chill went through her veins as he began to draw a handgun from behind his back.

"Sawyer!"

Before she could think, before she could run, Ella heard the familiar sound of a gun being cocked just behind her, and then her father's gruff voice telling her to step aside.

But Sawyer had this. With impressive swiftness and a few well-placed punches, Sawyer had his brother pinned to the wall with the gun at Richard's throat. Everyone stood frozen for what felt like forever and then finally Sawyer stepped back and let his brother go.

Not until Richard was at least thirty feet away from him did Sawyer lower the gun.

Her father lowered his too. "Why aren't you wearing your cloak?"

"Why are you even here?"

"Ray phoned. Said someone had been sniffing around the bunkhouse after Sawyer. He didn't like the look of him."

"Neither did I."

"Are you sure this is the one you want, Ella? You could just walk away. No one would fault you."

"You didn't teach me to walk away."

They watched in silence as Sawyer's brother walked unsteadily back toward the hotel, toward her father's pickup.

Her father began to raise his gun again and Ella stayed him with her hand. "If Cameron wants to stop him from leaving, he will."

"Did he threaten you?"

"He liked my feathers."

They watched some more as Sawyer's brother got in the pickup and drove away. Ella's father sighed.

"That was way too easy," Ella said. "Did you leave the keys in it?"

"Habit."

The sheriff came through the hotel doors and headed toward them, handing Ella back the phone without comment. Moments later, Sawyer walked up, shedding his jacket and draping it around Ella's shoulders. His brother's gun was no longer on show. Probably a good thing. Sawyer eyed her narrowly. "Didn't I tell you to stay inside?"

"Like that was ever going to work. Notice that I didn't interfere."

"I'm still a little unclear as to whether this guy's even within my jurisdiction, but I'll do my best," said the sheriff. "Lawyers and their double speak. Where is he?"

"I want to report a stolen vehicle," said Samuel T. Emerson.

And the good sheriff smiled.

SAWYER'S ENCOUNTER WITH his brother had left him with a faraway expression and a frown between his eyes. He didn't seem to be riding the adrenaline high of having a gun pulled on him or of disabusing his brother of that notion with a force that was all his own. Maybe he'd done this kind of thing before. Maybe he hid his disquiet well. Ella took his hand in hers and turned it over, looking for damage.

"I'm fine, Ella."

Maybe on the outside. "Do you want to go after him?"

"No, I—no. But I should."

"Or you could let the authorities do what they do best and leave it to them. Do you waltz?"

He looked at her, his gaze faintly incredulous.

"He came here looking to ruin your evening." Maybe he'd come here with even grimmer intentions, but Ella didn't want to dwell on that. She squeezed his hand lightly and bumped shoulders with him instead. "Do we really want to give him the satisfaction of having done so? I don't think so."

Sawyer laughed. It was only a little laugh, but it was there.

"Ella Grace Emerson, would you care to dance?"

"Why, thank you, kind sir, I'd love to."

He was light on his feet and he made her look graceful as they whirled around the dance floor beneath a ceiling of fairy light stars. He'd done this before. Not until he'd slowed and pulled her in close for movement sweet and slow did Ella tear her gaze from his to see what others thought. Her friend Joanne stood watching them with the biggest smile in her eyes. Reese Kendrick had a half hitch to his lips that for him equated to a broad smile. Jasper Flint was eyeing them with an air of quiet calculation and so was Jane from the chamber of commerce. Ella lifted her chin: let them calculate all they liked. Ella was exactly where she wanted to be and no-one, well-meaning or otherwise, was going to take that away from her.

She turned her gaze back to Sawyer, to those brilliant

green eyes and the smile in them, and the dimples in his cheeks, and felt blessed.

"I don't know how it happened," she murmured. "But all he's done is to make me want you more."

"That's 'cause you're ornery."

And then a smiling young woman thrust a piece of paper in between them. Several pieces of paper, stapled together. An entry form, no less. For The Great Wedding Giveaway. "We're a little low on entries so we're giving them out to likely-looking couples," she said. "And you two look gorgeous together. Love the dimples. And the dress." And then the smiling cupid was gone.

"We should enter," said Ella impulsively. "No, wait. Does that mean I just proposed to you?"

"Pretty much."

"Then I take it back."

"You don't want to propose to me?"

"Absolutely not. I want *you* to propose to *me.*"

"We should enter," Sawyer said, dimples and all. "And support Marietta's fine endeavor." Sawyer's delicious rumble held the teasing edge she'd come to love. "Help me fill it out."

Ella found her little clutch purse which had a pen in it, and then they found a shadowed corner of the ballroom's bar and dispensed with names and addresses, nationalities and dates of birth – the easy parts. When Ella stared at the blank lines where those five hundred loving words were supposed to go, she took a deep breath. To hell with supporting the town, it had all started with lust.

I saw him and my body said I want that, she wrote and then handed the pen to Sawyer.

I saw her and smiled.

"That's it? That's all you've got?" she asked and Sawyer rolled his eyes and added some more.

I saw her and smiled. She smiled right back and I trembled.

He handed her back the pen.

I spent time with him and my heart soared.

I got to know her and I couldn't stay away.

I saw the hunger in him, and the strength, and wanted more.

I shared my deepest fears with her and she kissed them away.

He remade his world for me and carved a place for me in it.

She shared her world with me and I gave her my heart.

I love you, and I don't want to win The Great Wedding Giveaway. It's a wonderful prize, but I can't wait that long when all I've ever dreamed of in a man is standing right in front of me. It's you, Cameron Franklin Sawyer. All that you are. All that we can be.

Elope with me.

No.

Marry me.

Yes.

She dropped the pen as he spun her into his arms and lifted her, kissed her, and, as always, the world around them faded away until there was only him. And lust. And a love so big it filled her heart to overflowing.

"I love you, Ella. With all that I am and all that I can be. I'm yours. Will you marry me?"

"Yes." Ella kissed him again, promptly lost herself once more in the warmth of him and the taste of forever. "Yes."

Chapter Ten

SIX WEEKS LATER Ella waited impatiently, two horses saddled and at the ready, as Sawyer drove up to the ranch and stepped from his pickup. He'd been in Australia for a little over a month helping his father refinance the family business, and he'd be going back again before he was through, but he'd kept his promise to return and Ella could barely wait for his smile and his touch.

This was what happened when wild longing turned into bone-deep love. You wanted a person to go and do what they had to do, you gave them your blessing and one-hundred-and-fifty percent of your support, and you vowed that when they came back you'd give them time to settle and room to breathe.

She'd been doing so *well* with all of that.

And then Sawyer set both feet on the ground and turned, and Ella launched herself into his arms, glorying in the way they closed tightly around her as he swept her off her feet. Video calls were wonderful things but they couldn't compete to having a living, breathing Sawyer in her arms, swinging her around, his deep laughter wrapping around her heart.

"You've no idea how much I've missed you," he muttered. "I couldn't wait to get back."

"I'm coming with you next time." Ella proceeded to lay kisses from his neck all the way to his temple. "You've no idea the number of people who are putting in for the ticket. Apparently I'm not all that good at patiently waiting for you to return."

"Who'd have guessed?" His voice slid through her, a deep delicious rumble shot through with laughter. "How would you feel about one month in Australia—one month here for a while?"

"I'd feel good." Better than good. And then his lips were on hers, strong and sure and the greeting turned into a homecoming as one kiss slid into the next, each one notching the heat up that little bit hotter until finally, for the sake of breathing room, Ella broke away.

"You keep kissing me like that and I'm likely to agree to anything."

His dimples put in an appearance as he smiled, which was just plain *mean* when it came to Ella retaining her decorum. "I know you've had a long trip, but how do *you* feel about heading up to the lodge tonight?" she asked him as he turned his head to eyeball the horses. "It's private and warm, I stocked it full of food yesterday afternoon and we can get as naked as we want there. Nakedness being a priority to my way of thinking. I want you stretched out in front of the log fire there. I've been dreaming up all sorts of variations on that particular theme. Long live the imagination, I say."

"How do the horses fit in?"

"They're for getting there. We can drive up the mountain as far as we can, and then take the horses from there. It shouldn't take too long. Okay, it might take a while. Especially if I have to teach you how to ride on the way. We can go slow. I'll probably die of anticipation on the way. You haven't changed your mind about wanting me, have you?" That last question came out so needy that she immediately wanted to take it back.

"Ella, are you babbling?"

"I don't babble." Much.

Could be she was a little nervous as to how Sawyer's time in Australia might have changed him. But he didn't look all that changed. His hair was a fraction tidier and his face looked a little bit more tanned, but the light in his eyes when he looked at her was just the same and his kisses felt as magical to her as ever. "Do you still want to marry me?"

He stepped back, set her at arms-length and eyed her sternly. "Ella Grace soon-to-be Sawyer, what kind of question is that?"

"A needy one," she admitted. "I just—"

"Yes," he interrupted gruffly. "Yes, I want to marry you. I even have a ring for you this time. There was a distinct lack of a ring last time we discussed this, as I recall. Maybe you're feeling that lack."

"You are so right. Let's put my neediness down to that. It's nothing at all to do with feeling achingly vulnerably head over heels in love with you."

He shared a smile made for soothing the skittish. "Would it help if I told you that I feel exactly the same way about you?"

"You should probably say that a lot."

"I will. Would you like your ring now or would you rather wait until there's a crackling fire in the background rather than two horses and several farm vehicles in the background?"

"Now. Definitely now," and then as an afterthought, "please."

Sawyer dug in his pocket and pulled out what looked like a scrap of black velvet. The material fell aside to reveal two rings, one a plain white band and the other ring considerably more ornate. It had three blindingly white diamonds set in a row across the band, all of them enormous. And that was before she took into account the scattering of smaller pink stones winding their way around the base of the others.

"Whoa!"

"So, was that a good *whoa*?"

It had definitely been an unladylike *whoa*. A lady would have aimed for a quietly pleased gasp. "Sawyer, it's gorgeous!"

"They're Kimberley diamonds." Sawyer slid the engagement ring on her finger and then brought her hand up and kissed the inside of her wrist. "Don't lose them in a cow."

"I would *never*. I'd go in after them."

His dimples put on a show. "Good to know."

"Shall we show my father?" Ella tilted her fingers this way and that, making the diamonds catch the light as Sawyer wrapped the wedding ring back in velvet and slid it in his pocket. "I think we should. And then he'll want to know what you've been doing this past month, and then he'll try and show you his new bull, to which you will say 'tomorrow' because if you go admiring bulls today we are never going to get away in time to make it to the lodge before nightfall."

"And that would be bad."

"Especially seeing as I want to take a couple of quick detours along the way to look at possible building sites for a safe and private little mountain cabin."

"Don't you already have one of those?"

He definitely had her measure. She favored him with her most angelic smile. "Or a sprawling family home. I've been talking with the grandson of the architect who built the ranch. He's a big fan of his grandfather's work and he has lots of ideas of his own. Fusion architecture. It sounds very appealing."

"I really shouldn't have left you alone for a month, should I?"

"So. Much. Time on my hands." She took his hand and tugged him towards the house. "Not that I'm impatient but the sooner you say hello to my father the sooner we can get away. He'll be happy to see you and he'll *really* like the ring. He can say I'm engaged if I have the ring."

"He really doesn't mind you marrying me, does he?"

"He knows what I want and he knows what I need, and you're it."

"My brother—"

"Is not you."

"—is likely to be in prison for quite some time, but he will get out one day."

"And if he comes for me and mine ever again he'll regret it. I protect what's mine."

"That's my line."

"I want a different line. A better one."

"I'll try and deliver it naked."

And off she went on yet another naked Sawyer-induced fantasy. "We probably only need five minutes or so with my father. Remember the lodge and the open fireplace? You naked amongst all the rugs? I would really like to remember it well and that won't happen if we don't actually get there. We're on a tight schedule, especially if we have to walk the horses through the snow to the lodge... and since you don't know how to ride."

He grinned wide and boyish as he glanced at the horses. "I know I don't know anything about cattle. I never said I couldn't ride."

"Have you been holding out on me, cowboy?"

"Not anymore and never again." He swung her into his arms again and Ella was only too willing to stay there. "I love you. I'm always going to love you, need you, care for you and want to be with you." He ducked his head, brushed his lips against the tender lobe of her ear and Ella whimpered with want and with need as heat unfurled low in her belly. "We are going to have the most amazing life together," he promised.

And she believed him.

Epilogue

F ROM THE BULLETIN board of Grey's Saloon, the pen of
Mardie Griffin, and accompanied by a snapshot of the
blissful bride being swept off her feet by the groom…

*Last Saturday, former bartender Cam Sawyer married
Marietta's own Ella Grace Emerson beneath a blue
summer sky and with the soaring Crazy Mountains of
Montana right behind them.*

*Ella was attended by Joanna Talbot and Mardie
Griffin, who loved their beautiful muted caramel-
colored gowns of silk and taffeta almost as much as they
loved their bridesmaid necklaces. General consensus has
it that both Jo and Mardie looked very fine indeed (both
Mardie and Joanna are currently seeking the perfect
lover and/or a domestic God of a husband).*

*One of the groom's attendants was a beautiful and
mysterious young Spanish woman, whose husband also
attended as a guest. The other groomsman was a childhood friend of Sawyer's named Joe.*

The groom's brother was not in attendance because

he's doing a nickel and dime, but the groom's parents were there, dressed to impress and looking rather pleased with the show. They have Ella for a daughter-in-law now – damn right they should be pleased.

The reception took place in the Emersons' ever-so-atmospheric and freshly painted and re-floored big barn. Rumor has it that Ella stole all the Graff Hotel's fairy lights for the occasion, but the Graff fairy lights are pink and Ella's were white and I have it on good authority that Ella purchased them herself, so... She probably purchased them in anticipation of all the future Emerson barn dances she's going to host for her dear single friends.

The quality of the beverages provided by the groom's parents had to be tasted to be believed. Maybe drinks spectacular was because JB Brewing is back on its feet now, with no small thanks to Sawyer, but I figure the elder Sawyers would have spent up big on their son's wedding anyway. His mother thinks Sawyer makes the sun rise. His father only thinks he hung the stars.

This isn't quite the case.

I know for a fact that Ella and her bridesmaids hung most of those shiny little stars while Sawyer was out somewhere delivering a calf with Samuel T.

The country and western band sounded absolutely brilliant, even if they did sometimes play the blues, and the dancing lasted until dawn. Coincidentally, this was around the time the bride and groom slipped away.

As the sky grew lighter, our very own bartender Josh took up one of the band member's guitars and showed us all how bluegrass should be played. He's so good, in fact, that our altogether taciturn Jason Grey waxed lyrical (his exact words were 'You're not bad') and then proceeded to offer Josh a Sunday afternoon solo gig at the saloon – for double pay.

I'm still trying to convince Reese that we need a Happy Hour then too, but that's an announcement for another day. Back to the wedding.

The big breakfast cook-up the next morning was a treat, and the gift boxes guests received on their way out the barn door contained complimentary coffee vouchers for several of Marietta's wonderful cafés and a selection of Sage's chocolates to devour on the drive back to town.

Congratulations, Ella and Sawyer, from your friends at Grey's Saloon. We love you both and wish you every magical, love-soaked moment this world possesses.

THE END

THE GREAT WEDDING GIVEAWAY

If you enjoyed *What a Bride Wants*, don't miss the other
Great Wedding Giveaway stories!

The Tycoon's Kiss by Jane Porter
Second Chance Bride by Trish Morey
Almost a Bride by Sarah Mayberry
The Unexpected Bride by Joanne Walsh
The Cowboy's Reluctant Bride by Katherine Garbera
The Tycoon's Bride by Megan Crane
The Substitute Bride by Kathleen O'Brien
Last Year's Bride by Anne McAllister
The Make-Believe Wedding by Sarah Mayberry

Available now at your favorite online retailer!

ABOUT THE AUTHOR

Accidentally educated in the sciences, Kelly Hunter didn't think to start writing romances until she was surrounded by the jungles of Malaysia for a year and didn't have anything to read. Kelly now lives in Australia, surrounded by lush farmland and family. Kelly is a USA Today bestselling author, a three-time RITA finalist and loves writing to the short contemporary romance form.

For more from Kelly, visit KellyHunter.co.

Thank you for reading

WHAT A BRIDE WANTS

If you enjoyed this book, you can find more from all our great authors at TulePublishing.com, or from your favorite online retailer.

40387402R00095